TARGET SEVEN

(THE SPY GAME—BOOK 7)

JACK MARS

Jack Mars

Jack Mars is the USA Today bestselling author of the LUKE STONE thriller series, which includes seven books. He is also the author of the new FORGING OF LUKE STONE prequel series, comprising six books; of the AGENT ZERO spy thriller series, comprising twelve books; of the TROY STARK thriller series, comprising five books; and of the SPY GAME thriller series, comprising nine books.

Jack loves to hear from you, so please feel free to visit www.Jackmarsauthor.com to join the email list, receive a free book, receive free giveaways, connect on Facebook and Twitter, and stay in touch!

ISBN: 978-1-0943-8380-4

BOOKS BY JACK MARS

THE SPY GAME
TARGET ONE (Book #1)
TARGET TWO (Book #2)
TARGET THREE (Book #3)
TARGET FOUR (Book #4)
TARGET FIVE (Book #5)
TARGET SIX (Book #6)
TARGET SEVEN (Book #7)
TARGET EIGHT (Book #8)
TARGET NINE (Book #9)

TROY STARK THRILLER SERIES
ROGUE FORCE (Book #1)
ROGUE COMMAND (Book #2)
ROGUE TARGET (Book #3)
ROGUE MISSION (Book #4)
ROGUE SHOT (Book #5)

LUKE STONE THRILLER SERIES
ANY MEANS NECESSARY (Book #1)
OATH OF OFFICE (Book #2)
SITUATION ROOM (Book #3)
OPPOSE ANY FOE (Book #4)
PRESIDENT ELECT (Book #5)
OUR SACRED HONOR (Book #6)
HOUSE DIVIDED (Book #7)

FORGING OF LUKE STONE PREQUEL SERIES
PRIMARY TARGET (Book #1)
PRIMARY COMMAND (Book #2)
PRIMARY THREAT (Book #3)
PRIMARY GLORY (Book #4)
PRIMARY VALOR (Book #5)
PRIMARY DUTY (Book #6)

AN AGENT ZERO SPY THRILLER SERIES
AGENT ZERO (Book #1)

TARGET ZERO (Book #2)
HUNTING ZERO (Book #3)
TRAPPING ZERO (Book #4)
FILE ZERO (Book #5)
RECALL ZERO (Book #6)
ASSASSIN ZERO (Book #7)
DECOY ZERO (Book #8)
CHASING ZERO (Book #9)
VENGEANCE ZERO (Book #10)
ZERO ZERO (Book #11)
ABSOLUTE ZERO (Book #12)

Dedicated to Julie Hayden, a beloved wife, mother, and grandmother.
An inspiration to everyone she met.

PROLOGUE

A hilltop five miles northeast of the village of Al Jaghbub
Eastern Libya
Dusk

Dr. Moswen Farag wiped the sweat from his brow and cursed the infidel who had plundered the ancient temple he stood in.

Dr. Farag did not care that a priceless artifact had been stolen. There was a time when the former Egyptologist would have been horrified. But he had seen the light, stepped onto Allah's true path of jihad, and now understood that the ancient things he had once admired were filthy relics of a debased society.

But the theft still brought his blood to a boil because he wanted to be the one to take it.

The middle-aged man wiped his brow again and looked around the dusty, windblown hilltop in eastern Libya, just a few miles from the Egyptian border. There wasn't much to see on the surface, just the stone foundations of a large temple ringed by a heap of rubble from where time had pulled down the walls, and a scattering of potsherds scattered on the sandy surface. Sand had filled the temple to the point that he knew he stood a good ten feet above the floor.

Even the holy warriors who had come with him, in the ignorance, could tell that, because at one end of the rectangular temple was a deep pit revealing a statue of Ra. His men had dug it under his direction.

But as they did so, his trained eye picked up a detail that made him worry.

He could clearly see the outlines of a filled-in pit right around where they were uncovering the statue. The sand had been sifted, had no artifacts in it, unlike the surrounding sand, and wasn't as tightly packed as the rest of the sand.

Someone had dug here and then refilled the hole. It had been a while ago because the sand had settled and grown packed, although not as packed as the sand that had laid undisturbed around it for millennia.

If that wasn't proof enough, in one spot he could see a clear outline between the two types of sand, a subtle shift that he could trace sloping downwards.

The side of the old pit.

He had told his men to continue digging anyway, hoping against hope, until they had revealed the statue of Ra to its full height.

Now that hope had vanished. Its staff was missing, taken in the 1940s.

And Dr. Farag knew who took it.

General Erwin Rommel had led his famous Afrika Korps through this region as he pushed toward the Suez Canal. He had brought along a team of archaeologists to search for ancient sites along the way. The Nazis had been obsessed with ancient civilizations, especially that of Ancient Egypt. Dr. Farag had hoped this site had eluded them.

Now he could see he was wrong.

Dr. Farag looked around, temporarily at a loss. The site had been more than just a temple. Surrounding it were more ruins, the remains of a fortress, and the small town that served it. A riverbed wound its meandering way along the eastern base of the hill. It would have once provided water to the outpost but had long since gone dry.

Dr. Farag shook his head. What bitter irony. When he was a younger and more foolish man, and loved the ancient pagan things, finding this place would have been the highlight of his career. He had figured out through obscure papyri and the latest satellite imagery that where he stood was the westernmost outpost of the Egyptian empire, built by the Pharaoh Senusret III in 1840 BC to guard the frontier against hostile Libyan tribes. It was similar to a site he had visited near the village of Ibn Balamon in the Sudan to guard the southern reaches of Egypt from the Nubians.

In his new life, finding the statue intact would have been the high point of his career, because the statue before him held a stone staff. Its front had been removed to reveal a hollow recess. Inside, he knew, would have been a lead cylinder filled with naturally occurring uranium-235.

He knew this because the ancients had discovered a natural source for such fissile material somewhere and had learned to use it as a weapon via the use of a crude collimator. They called it the 'withering power of Ra'.

There had been an identical statue, with an identical hidden core, at Ibn Balamon in the Sudan. He had discovered it. He had safely put the core in a sealed carrying case and was ready to leave when that American bitch of an archaeologist had swooped in with her CIA friend, killed half his crew, and took it from him.

Jana Peters. He had plans for her.

But first, he needed to make The Sword of the Righteous a nuclear power.

"So what do we do?" a voice behind him asked.

He turned and saw Hamza, his righthand man, a hulk of a fellow with small eyes set close together under a beetling brow. An excellent fighter, dedicated to the cause, and smarter than the average run of Allah's warriors he had assembled, although that wasn't saying much. The team stood at various points on the ancient site, keeping watch for wandering Bedouin or herders from the nearby village.

At least they didn't have to worry about the local militia, one of many in Libya's ongoing civil war. He had already paid them off.

The Sword of the Righteous had deep pockets, thanks to a brilliant heist of artifacts from the Louvre, artifacts they had been selling back to the infidel French one by one.

A good thing, too, because only deep pockets would solve their problem now.

"We must do what the Englishman asks," he told Hamza. "It's clear now that he really has it."

"Why don't we just kill him?" Hamza growled.

Dr. Farag tried to contain his impatience. Killing was, after all, what Hamza did best. "Because that would attract attention, and that is the last thing we want. We need time to make the device. We are hunted enough as it is. Our enemies will be on the lookout for anyone associated with the antiquities trade dying or disappearing."

"We could kidnap him, have him call his family and say he went on a long trip."

Dr. Farag shook his head. "No, brother. We have enough to pay him. If he was clever enough to track it down on the black market and buy it, he will be clever enough to keep the Staff of Ra hidden, and to have tight security measures in place in case he's abducted."

A small part of him felt relieved. Radiation unsettled him, and while they had come equipped with Tyvek suits and a lead case in which to put the large cylinder of uranium, none of them were professionals at handling radioactive material. The staff in the Sudan had been leaking, and he felt sure he had gotten a dose of radiation despite keeping his distance and letting his men do the digging. The thought of the invisible rays disrupting his DNA and ravaging his cell structure gave him the shivers.

"I don't want to hand millions over the some unbeliever so he can drink whiskey and sleep with whores," Hamza growled.

"It is of no matter. We have the money. His reckoning will come one day."

Hamza smiled. "I hope I am that reckoning."

Dr. Farag put a hand on his shoulder. "I hope so too, and I hope you film it. You know how much we like your videos."

A shout from one of the sentries on the southern edge of the hill made them whirl around.

"What is it?" Hamza demanded, already unslinging the Kalashnikov from his back.

"A flare of light, brother, from the southeast. I think it was a pair of binoculars."

Dr. Farag and Hamza ran over, the younger man easily outpacing the academic.

By the time Dr. Farag caught up, huffing and puffing, Hamza and the sentry were kneeling behind the remains of an ancient wall, peering out over the rough landscape. Dr. Farag followed their gaze and saw nothing but bare stones and sand.

"There, sir," the sentry said, pointing. "In the cleft on that far hill."

Dr. Farag squinted. "I don't see anything."

"It was there."

He didn't doubt it. Dr. Farag had only brought his best warriors along.

"Who could it be?" he asked.

Hamza scratched his stubble and said, "From that direction, it's either the Egyptian army or the militia."

While the border was ten kilometers to the east through harsh and barren desert, it wasn't unknown for Egyptian scouting units to probe into Libya to monitor the many factions in the country's civil war. Several jihadist groups made Libya their home and sometimes launched attacks on Egypt's regime.

The Egyptians deserved it. The military junta licked the boots of the West and allowed Egypt's Christian community to exist. They would get their judgment one day.

Or could it be the militia, spying on them? They couldn't be thinking of double-crossing them, could they? No, they had no reason to do so. There was no profit in it.

Then a third possibility arose in his mind.

The CIA.

Dr. Farag bit his lower lip. He had barely made it out of that firefight in the Sudan alive, and he had had a much larger force then. With the international manhunt going on, he had been forced to flee to flee to Yemen for a time and had only at great risk to himself snuck back into Egypt to make it here with a small force that had set out in ones and twos before rendezvousing at a remote spot at the border.

A shadow passed over the land. The sun had gone behind a distant mountain. Soon, the dark desert night would cloak their movements.

"Get ready to head out," Dr. Farag said.

Hamza nodded. "Yes, sir. We'll go down the opposite side of this hill and work our way north for a time until it's fully dark before cutting east to the border."

Dr. Farag always felt a nettling sense of annoyance when Hamza made decisions without consulting him, but held his tongue. The warrior knew far more about these matters than he did.

And this mission was far too important to let his ego get in the way. For if they could buy the Staff of Ra from that English collector, and combine it with the smaller priest's staff from Karnak already in his possession, he would have just over the threshold of 50 kilos of fissile material needed to make a nuclear device.

He had an engineering team ready and waiting. They had the bomb already made; they only needed the uranium-235.

And then it was only a matter of smuggling the bomb into the most convenient Western city, setting it off, and taking responsibility. That would start a war between Islam and the West. The unbelieving nations would unleash hell on the Muslim nations, rallying the entire Islamic world to the banner of jihad. The long war would drain the West's strength to the point that Islam, true Islam, would prevail.

So yes, he would sneak back across the border and make arrangements to buy the Libyan Staff of Ra from the Englishman. The price would be steep, it might mean selling a couple of more artifacts back to the French, but the French had proven willing to pay and the Englishman was motivated solely by greed.

It would all work out, and within a month, The Sword of the Righteous would be picking its target.

Dr. Farag smiled as his men loaded up their gear and together they scrambled down the north slope of the hill, keeping to a narrow gorge that hid them from view.

He had another project in the works as well, and Allah willing it would soon come to fruition.

Exacting a terrible revenge on Jana Peters.

CHAPTER ONE

Paris
The next evening

Jana Peter sat back in her chair and enjoyed a feeling that had become almost alien to her—inner peace.

She knew this feeling was only temporary, a fleeting respite between harrowing episodes of danger, and that made it all the more enjoyable.

Because the Sword of the Righteous wasn't defeated yet. Dr. Moswen Farag had escaped with ten kilos of fissile material in the Karnak Staff of Ra.

All the forces of the Egyptian secret service, helped by the CIA, the UK's MI6, and France's Direction Générale de la Sécurité Extérieure, had been scouring the globe for him for a month, but so far he had eluded them.

He was a crafty opponent, and had obviously planned his escape beforehand. Chatter had gone dead, known terror cells had scattered, informants had nothing to offer. It was as if The Sword of the Righteous had simply vanished.

Jana knew better.

Still, she felt relaxed. She was home. She was reading in one of the great libraries of Europe—the Bibliothèque nationale de France in Paris.

Even more, she sat in the great "Salle ovale", the grand oval reading room with its elegant sweep of bookshelves beneath an encircling row of arches ringing the room, and above a series of round windows and an enormous skylight held up by an intricate spider's web of ironwork.

Those were beautiful when the sun streamed through, doubly beautiful with the moon shining.

It was late, but Jana didn't care. She sat at a spacious wooden desk illuminated by a green glass reading lamp. Before her were stacks of French archaeological reports from the late nineteenth and early twentieth centuries, covering expeditions to Egypt and the Sudan. This library had the greatest Egyptological collection in the world for early French reports.

It used to be second best, after the Institut d'Égypte in Cairo, but that got torched during the Arab Spring in 2011. Not everyone valued the treasure that was a library.

Jana Peters sure did. She had studied in some of the best, and they were all adventures in and of themselves. The ornate 15th century Duke Humfrey's Library in Oxford, the massive Library of Congress in Washington, DC, and the National Library of Ethiopia in Addis Ababa, housed in one of Haile Selassie's old palaces, where the reading room was a converted ballroom and Jana did her research under a painted ceiling and vast crystal chandelier.

The Bibliothèque nationale de France could compete with the best of them. Founded in 1461, its exterior looked like some grand French palace of Louis XIV, and its interior had two vast, echoing floors of marble and high, columned ceilings with two dozen reading rooms. Its holdings were some of the largest in the world.

And what holdings! She had spent the whole day and a good part of the evening poring over rare publications not available anywhere else. Not even in online academic databases. Most of the older texts had never been digitalized and probably never would, given the vastness of the material.

And she needed these yellowing old pages with their carefully crafted etchings and their grainy black and white photos. They contained a lot of discoveries that had since been lost—smaller or briefly surveyed sites that no one had ever returned to and had never made it into the modern databases.

She was working on a theory that the Temple of Ra in the Sudan wasn't the only one. It had been set in a fortress, and with its radioactive staff and crude collimator, the statue of the sun god could be used as a weapon, although one almost as dangerous to the wielder as the enemy.

The Egyptians were meticulous, and worked in an orderly, repetitive fashion. If they had built a temple to Ra on one frontier, they would have built similar ones on the other frontiers.

That meant Libya, where the ancient Egyptians had been in constant battle with the various tribes there, and Sinai, where the Egyptians had to contend with the Israelites, Canaanites, and later the Assyrians and Babylonians.

The location of the Libyan temple would have most likely been close to Siwa Oasis in Egypt's western desert, Siwa being the last outpost of their civilization, or perhaps along the shore, where there was a denser population thanks to more arable land. Perhaps there were temples in both locations.

Locating the Sinai temple was trickier. The border there had fluctuated, sometimes being on the western edge of the peninsula where the Suez Canal now stood, sometimes on the eastern edge of the peninsula. At times, Egypt controlled Israel, so the frontier would have been much further to the northeast.

She tried to think like Dr. Farag. He wanted to find an intact statue of Ra while bringing the least amount of attention on himself.

That ruled out the Sinai and Israel. The Egyptian and Israeli armies were on constant high alert in those regions, and being on the run, Dr. Farag would not want to risk going there.

She had scoured the literature anyway, and while she had found a couple of temples to Ra in roughly the right place, neither had a large statue of the deity holding a staff. If there had been a temple there, it must have been thoroughly destroyed in antiquity. There had been so many excavations in the region that surely such a big site would have been discovered long ago.

That left the Egyptian/Libyan border. For the past five hours, she had been going through old reports for that region.

At first, she had concentrated on the coastal region. Sadly, there wasn't much. From 1911 to the outbreak of World War Two, Libya had been an Italian colony, and France's national library was a bit thin on Italian publications. She found no evidence of any Egyptian temples to Ra or any frontier forts that weren't fully excavated in more recent decades.

She turned to the more inland region, thinking that a working vacation in Rome might be in order. Jacob sure wouldn't mind the food. French *haute cuisine* was a bit too refined for him. She knew this little trattoria in near Santa Maria Maggiore that he'd love.

Jana stopped making up romantic scenes with her very unromantic companion (friend? Boyfriend? Who knew?) and got back to work.

After another couple of hours, she struck gold, or at least thought she might have.

Oddly, it came in one of the most recent publications she had looked at, an article in a military journal by a French archaeology student based in Cairo at the time of the Nazi invasion of France.

Unable to make it to his homeland to help in its defense, and unable to get in contact with the Free French forces who had fled to England, he joined the Commonwealth Army instead. Thanks to his knowledge of the land and the language, he was more than welcome. He ended up with the Sixth Australian Division fighting first the Italians, and then against the Afrika Korps.

One day in December of 1940, he and his unit went out on a scouting mission near the village of Al Jaghbub in eastern Libya, where an Italian army was camped around the oasis there, and made an unusual discovery. On a hilltop a few kilometers away, not far west of the Egyptian border, he had found extensive ruins, both of large stone blocks and of mudbrick. Potsherds and a few fragmentary inscriptions on the surface told him the site was Egyptian. He had traced the foundations and posited that it was a fortress complex with a large temple. Being on active duty, he only got to search the site for an hour and make a crude sketch that he included in the article.

It looked an awful lot like the fortress and temple complex in the Sudan.

Sadly, the Frenchman never got a chance to go back to the site. The Australian forces encircled the Italian base shortly thereafter and put it under siege. After three months of fighting, the Italians surrendered. The Frenchman's unit then advanced to the west along with the rest of the Commonwealth troops. He was never able to return to the site he had discovered.

She noted the site's position and decided to ask Jacob to pull up some military satellite imagery of it. Given how the region was a hotbed of terrorist activity right next to one of America's few reliable Middle Eastern allies, they were sure to have mapped the whole area in minute detail. He might even be able to ask for a special viewing from one of the spy satellites.

She yawned and stretched. Time to call it a night. She'd delve further into the archives tomorrow, but for now she had made enough progress. Time for a glass of wine and a moonlit stroll through Paris with Jacob.

As she stretched, movement out of the corner of her eye caught her attention.

Ever since Jacob had come into her life, Jana had become a lot more aware of her surroundings. Her father had taught her plenty of survival skills when she was a girl, but she had never had much cause to use them until she got swept up into the world of international espionage and counterterrorism.

At this hour the library was mostly empty, the professors having gone home to their families, the students off to dates and dinner, leaving only a few hardcore researchers like her.

No one sat close to her. In the whole vast reading room, she could see maybe five or six readers, although there might have been more in the upper tiers or hidden by the columns. Certainly not more than a dozen in total.

One guy had caught her eye. A younger French guy, maybe in his early thirties, he sat to her right at a desk facing her, working his way through a stack of old leather-bound volumes. He had been there almost as long as she had.

Jana had caught him looking up at her a couple of times. That might just mean he was a pervert, or it could mean he was a lot worse.

While not getting paranoid, Jana had remained aware of him all through the day and into the evening.

And now he was walking along the row of desks at which she sat, carrying a folder of papers that seemed to bulge suspiciously in the middle. If he kept coming, he'd pass right behind her.

There was no reason for him to come this way. The bathrooms, exit, and librarian counter all lay in other directions.

Jana pretended to reach for another book, which just happened to let her turn a little more in his direction without appearing to do so deliberately.

She made a half-second assessment and decided his build, carriage, and confidence did not speak of a graduate student or young professor. No, he moved with the ease and grace of a trained fighter, and his eyes roved all over the room, as if checking for witnesses.

That put Jana on the alert, and when she glanced his way again as he drew closer, it allowed her to jump into action.

Because just as he got within two steps of her, he dropped the folder he had been carrying to reveal a combat knife.

Jana picked up the heaviest volume on her desk and flung it at his face. He knocked it away with lightning reflexes and dove for her.

Oh dear, the pen isn't mightier than the sword.

Jana threw herself onto the floor to the left of her chair, and the knife slashed only air.

She kicked the chair at him, and in the second it took him to untangle himself, she was on her feet and running.

The sound of pursuit, interspersed with a couple of gasps from other readers. Most academics weren't accustomed to seeing one of their colleagues getting chased through the library by a knife-wielding maniac.

She bolted down the row of desks, grabbing chairs and tossing them in her pursuer's path. He leaped over them like he was doing hurdles in the Olympics. They barely slowed him down. In fact, he was gaining on her.

Jana jagged to the left, where several rows of bookshelves gave her a chance to duck out of sight. She took a right, took the first left she could, and crouched low, hoping to hide herself in the stacks.

Nope. He was too close to her and spotted her through gaps in the books. He rounded the corner, knife held low, and she had to bolt again, running so fast she didn't have the lung capacity to scream for help. Hopefully one of the gaping academics would have enough presence of mind to call security.

This time she made for a spiral ironwork staircase near the wall. She got on it, thundering up the stairs and hoping the noise she made would bring more attention to her plight.

The assassin came right after her, barely a turn of the staircase behind. Once again, he started to gain ground.

Time for another change of plan. She spun, grabbed the railing, and as he came around, she lifted herself off the steps and lashed out with both feet.

Her right foot caught him square in the face. He staggered back, grasped the railing, and just managed not to fall.

Jana got back on her feet, ready to attack again, and saw him recovering too quickly.

She ran up the rest of the stairs and into the labyrinth of bookshelves on the upper floor.

Those would hide her, but not for long. Maybe not long enough for help to come.

At least help was just around the corner.

She got to a spot on the aisle where lots of tall volumes crammed the shelves, helping obscure her from view, crouched down, and pulled out her phone.

She texted Jacob with a single-word message.

"SOS."

CHAPTER TWO

Jacob Snow sat in a brasserie just around the corner from the library, enjoying some fine French wine. Usually, he preferred whiskey, but the guy behind the counter had turned up his Gallic nose when he asked for some. Apparently asking for a single malt Scotch in an expensive bar in Paris was considered gauche.

Screw him. He needed to find a decent British pub somewhere in town where a man could get a man's drink. If he was in Greece, he could order ouzo. The bartender here had offered him absinthe, but the memory of a bad absinthe night many years ago with his Ranger buddies made him say no. He didn't want to end up having to be bailed out of jail for beating up an entire Portuguese soccer team. Once was enough for one lifetime.

So he sat at ease sipping what he had to admit was some excellent white wine, surveying the bar from his spot with his back to the wall, near the rear emergency exit, while facing the entrance.

Jacob Snow always sat with his back to the wall facing the entrance, and finding the other way out of a building was the first thing he did upon entering it.

He wished Jana was here. She'd appreciate this hoity toity place a lot more than he did. Mood lighting. Brass fittings. Classical music. Inflated prices. Having someone with a few social graces around would sure make the evening better. And he had just had a plate of steamed oysters, so he could use some feminine company.

Sitting at the bar was a beautiful French brunette of about twenty-five who looked like she wanted to volunteer. She'd been eyeing him over a glass of champagne for some time now.

He ignored her attempts to catch his eye. His heart was already called for, even though it was still in grief over his last lover.

Gabriella had been killed just a few months before in a hit directed at him. The guilt over that would, he knew, stay with him forever.

And it was not lessened by finding love with Jana, a woman he thought he'd never have in his life even as an acquaintance, let alone a fellow counterterrorism operative and lover.

The Frenchwoman smiled at him, then leaned over and whispered something to the bartender.

Sorry, lady. You don't want to get close to me. For several reasons. Actually, for a whole bunch of reasons.

After a minute, the bartender came over to him with another glass of wine.

"Compliments of the lady at the bar," he said.

Jacob raised the glass to her in a toast and got a sultry look in return.

Uh-oh. Maybe I should wear a wedding band like some women do.

The woman returned the toast, then rose. She walked toward him, her black silk dress sliding over her delicious curves and graceful movements.

Jacob's throat suddenly felt dry. He took a slug of wine for courage and tried to think of a polite way to turn her down. Courtesy was not Jacob Snow's strong point.

Luckily he didn't need to think of something nice to say, because just then his cell phone saved him.

It buzzed with the tone reserved for Jana.

He pulled out his phone quicker than Clint Eastwood drawing a sixgun and leapt to his feet.

The message said only "SOS."

He switched to locate. Their phones were tethered to always show each other's location.

She was still in the library, and she was in trouble.

Jacob dropped the glass and bolted past the woman, her shout of surprise and the shattering of glass breaking the mood of the brasserie simultaneously.

He burst out of the front door, nearly bowling over an elderly couple coming in, and pelted down the street.

The national library stood just around the corner. Cutting across the intersection, dodging a truck only to nearly get taken out by a moped, he made it there in twenty seconds flat.

Even at nine o'clock at night, the place was still open, although he saw no one standing around the front.

He hauled open the ornate brass door and rushed inside the marble lobby. There was a metal detector at the front, manned by a security guard in a baggy uniform who looked like he was about three weeks away from retirement.

Jacob blew past him and set off the metal detector as he passed through.

Oops. Guess that was because of the 9mm in my shoulder holster.

Next, he came to a turnstile where library members had to scan their cards. He vaulted over this and ran down a hallway toward the center of the building. Jana had mentioned that she'd be sitting in the library's central reading room, and the locator indicated she was still there.

He burst through the double doors into a beautiful oval reading room with two levels of walkways beneath a glass dome. Ahead of him stretched several rows of reading desks. Several academic types were clustered together, looking at one corner of the library. At the sound of him coming in, they turned in his direction.

"What's going on?" he demanded.

They all stared at him.

"English, people! You must have twelve PhDs between you. Someone must speak English!"

A scrawny man with tortoiseshell glasses pointed a thin arm.

"A man chased a woman over there."

"And you didn't go help?"

"I called the librarian."

"Useless!"

Jacob rushed to where the idiot had pointed. He saw a cluster of bookshelves and a spiral staircase of antique ironwork going up to the next level and then the one above that.

A thump upstairs told him the action had already made it off the ground floor.

"Call the police!"

Not that they'll get here in time.

He yanked out his gun, making Mr. Tortoise Shell Glasses screech a couple of octaves higher than what was acceptable for a male of the species, and rushed to the corner of the reading room.

Several more thumps sounded from upstairs before he made it to the spiral staircase. It sounded like books being dumped on the floor. Or on someone.

Was Jana fighting someone with books?

Typical.

Jacob took the stairs three at a time, banging against the railing a couple of times in his haste to make it to the next floor. He took a quick glance around and saw no one.

Running feet above him told him where to go.

Again he hurried up the old stairs, which rattled way more than he'd like.

He got up to the next story just in time to see Jana duck around a bookshelf about twenty feet down the nearest aisle. He didn't think she had seen him.

Everything went silent.

He paused, listening, knowing that Jana and her assailant (assailants?) were doing the same.

Jacob eased over to the next aisle and, leading with his gun, took a peek.

A bunch of books lay scattered along the aisle. Jana had picked the heaviest volumes. Jacob doubted they did more than slow her attacker down.

He noticed one book with a slashed cover.

Tsk tsk. Someone's going to get a fine.

Jacob crept to the next aisle, saw no one, and began to tiptoe down it.

He made no sound as he moved down the aisle, and whoever else was up here didn't make any noise either.

Unless he was missing it, thanks to those dumbasses babbling downstairs. Someone had just banged open a door, and an old voice shouted something in French. Probably that security guard he had breezed past.

But then he felt the hairs on his neck go up. A tingling sensation went through his body.

Anyone with combat experience knows and respects the sixth sense. Some think it's psychic, or God telling you to watch out. The more pragmatic say it's the subconscious picking up on sensations below the threshold of conscious awareness. The faintest sounds. A subtle new odor. Even the slightest variation in the ambient temperature.

Whatever the explanation, Jacob whirled around, crouching, aiming before he even knew what he was aiming at.

A lean, muscular man in his late twenties was a few feet behind him, wielding a knife made of sharpened, high-density ceramic, perfect for sneaking past metal detectors.

The knifeman stopped short, eyes going wide.

Jacob chuckled and stood.

“Remember Sean Connery’s line? ‘Never bring a knife to a gunfight.’”

The assassin’s hand moved lightning fast. The knife flew at him in a deadly blur, too fast to dodge.

Inches before the knife would have plunged into Jacob's chest, a book flew off the shelves, and the knife struck it with a *thunk*. The force of the thrown blade was enough to carry the book all the way to Jacob.

The sensation of a book hitting him was a lot more welcome than that of a knife.

The fist that came right afterward was a lot less welcome.

It hit Jacob square on the jaw, snapping his head back. A moment later he felt a flare of pain as a karate chop to the wrist of his gun hand made him drop the weapon.

Jacob staggered back, launched a front kick his opponent easily dodged, then blocked another punch aimed at his head.

Then it became a blur of motion. Attack, block, counterattack. Jacob took a gut punch, ducked a couple more blows, and then replied with a calf kick that nearly took the guy down.

He retreated, Jacob advanced, stepping on his own gun. He resisted the urge to try and get it. This guy was way too quick to pull a rookie move like that.

Especially when he retaliated with a calf kick of his own.

Right on the leg, standing on the gun.

Jacob staggered, heard a metallic *clunk* as the gun flew away and hit something, and then it was back to punching and blocking.

This guy was good. A combo of karate and Jiu-Jitsu. Might be on the semipro MMA circuit.

Good thing the aisle was too narrow for him to try out his floor game. Jacob had never done enough Judo or wrestling to compete with an MMA fighter.

Looked like he didn’t need to. Just as he took another sock to the jaw, he spotted Jana creeping up behind the assassin, wielding one of those little metal stools on wheels libraries had to help readers reach the upper shelves.

She raised it high, ready to bring it down hard on the guy’s head.

It was at this point that Grandpa the Security Guard decided to make an appearance.

He popped into the aisle right behind Jana and shouted, “Arrête!”

The assassin launched a front kick to make Jacob back off and glanced behind him just as Jana brought the stool down.

He blocked it, grunting in pain as it hit his forearms, then twisted it out of her grasp and tossed it at Jacob, who had to duck.

He rose up just in time to see the guy grab Jana, soak up an elbow she drove into his face, lift her up, and turn her upside down.

Jesus, is he going to do a pile driver?

Flashy in professional wrestling. Potentially fatal in real life.

Jacob kicked him in the back of the knee. The guy buckled, dropped his prey rather than slamming her into the floor, and grabbed the bookshelf to recover.

Jacob gave him a hefty punch in the face.

That was the last punch he got to give, because just then Grandpa the Security Guard doused the entire aisle in pepper spray.

Jacob had been facing him, so he got a direct spray into his eyes and mouth.

Coughing and tearing up, he tried to focus on what was going on with the hitman and Jana, but another dose of pepper spray made that impossible.

Lowering his head, Jacob charged forward. He tripped over someone and rammed right into a body too hard to be anyone's but the hitman's. An elbow rammed into his stomach. For a moment, Jacob stood doubled over, wiping his eyes with one hand and holding his stomach with the other.

Once he managed enough strength to look up, his body wracked with pain and coughing, he saw the killer plough through the security guard and run around the corner.

Jacob followed, half-blind and unable to run because he couldn't stop coughing. The guy had had his back turned to the security guard when the pepper spray went off, so he hadn't gotten as bad of a dose. That meant he easily outpaced Jacob as he headed for the stairs.

Jacob ducked to the right and went down an aisle of books that led to the staircase, coming out on the other side just in time to cut him off.

The killer stopped, backpedaled, and ran right for the railing overlooking the reading room. Jacob went after him.

His quarry was far too fast. He made it to the railing, looked down, and after only a moment's hesitation vaulted over.

A cry and a loud thump from below.

Jacob rushed to the railing and looked down, just in time to see through teary eyes the killer leap up from a small crowd of readers who had clustered below to watch the fight upstairs and who were now all lying on the floor, half unconscious.

The killer had used them to land on. Now, he was rushing to the door.

Jacob ran to the stairs and hurried down it, noticing with relief that Jana was staggering toward him, stunned and coughing but otherwise unhurt.

He knew he wasn't going to catch the assassin, but he ran after him anyway. This guy was too much of a pro and had too great of a lead. But who knew? Maybe luck would intervene.

Luck didn't, and by the time Jacob got downstairs and out the front door of the building, the man he had fought was nowhere to be seen.

He stood in front of the library, coughing and wiping his eyes. Jacob would put out a search with the Paris police and talk to the CIA, but he knew those searching would probably come up empty.

The Sword of the Righteous had put out a hit on Jana, and they were very skilled at disappearing when they needed to.

Or maybe it had been The Order. They had abducted her once before. Now maybe they were shifting their tactics and simply trying to killer her.

The question was—how the hell did they know Jana was in Paris? How did they know she would be studying at the national library? Only the CIA and French intelligence knew that.

Maybe both organizations had a lot better intel than anyone had given them credit for.

CHAPTER THREE

Sousse, on the Tunisian coast
That same day

Aaron Peters walked along the beach, looking for all the world like your typical tourist. He wore a bathing suit and flip-flops, and a sky blue bucket hat, one size too small, covered his head. A fanny pack completed the ensemble.

Any casual observer would take him for a goofy American enjoying a stroll on the beautiful beaches of Tunisia's most popular resort. A second look would pick up the weathered face and the muscled frame impressively filling out an "I love Tunisia" t-shirt he'd bought from a street vendor the previous day.

What they couldn't see were the eyes behind a pair of sunglasses, constantly searching the beach and the crowd on it. Those cold blue eyes picked up every detail. They saw which of the hundreds of European men and women on this beach were drunk or stoned and which were sober. They saw which of the many young Tunisian men selling sea shells or cold drinks were also scoping out who they could pickpocket. They saw the beach homes and resorts set beyond the dunes and noticed every good vantage point for a sniper.

Looking out to sea, Aaron Peters spotted the kite surfers enjoying the stiff Mediterranean breeze, a Tunisian Coast Guard cutter in the distance, and the fishing trawlers beyond it. Those eyes never stopped searching.

Searching for the bomb.

Intel he'd picked up had led him to believe there would be a bomb attack on this beach today. Tunisia had kept out of the numerous fights between the Western Powers and those of radical Islam. The Tunisian government had clamped down on Islamists and presented the nation as a friendly tourist destination, safe but exotic.

Except for a few attacks, including in Sousse a decade before, that was mostly true. The Tunisian national character didn't lend itself to radicalism. While there were Islamist groups in the country, they were small, and many of their rank and file were foreigners sneaking over the porous border from Libya.

But Aaron wasn't looking for some local Islamist group. He was looking for agents from The Order.

And that was an organization far, far more dangerous than some angry band of Muslim radicals.

The Order had tentacles in every important country in the world and operatives in dozens of law enforcement and intelligence agencies. It had eyes and ears everywhere, and more than once had come close to killing him.

It was Aaron Peters' sworn duty to wipe them out.

So far, he'd only given them a few black eyes. He wasn't even close to defeating them.

Still, he planned on inflicting another black eye today, and save a bunch of lives in the process.

If only he could find the damn bomb …

The best place to look was somewhere it could inflict maximum casualties. That ruled out the beach itself, where the openness of the terrain would reduce the force of the blast. Better to blow it up inside, in one of the many restaurants lining the beach.

But it was late afternoon, and most customers were sitting on the terraces to enjoy the pleasant weather. Once again an open target that would not give a satisfactory body count. He needed someplace inside, but who would stay inside on a nice day like this?

Then up ahead he found his answer. One of the resort town's top nightclubs, The Jewel Lounge, had set up an outside dance floor.

It measured about thirty feet to a side, raised a couple of feet above the sand. A DJ booth was set up to one side, and an open bar on the other. Drinking was allowed in Tunisia for non-Muslims, although drinking in public like this was frowned upon by most locals.

The DJ must have been someone popular because the dance floor was packed with a couple of hundred young people, almost all foreign.

A perfect target.

Another detail made this spot even more likely.

There was a fringe of black cloth all around the dance floor emblazoned with the nightclub's logo, entirely blocking the view beneath.

If someone could get in there undetected, they could take their sweet time setting up a bomb, and no one would see them, and certainly no one would hear them.

The *thud thud thud* of the House music kept time with Aaron's heart as he approached. He noticed a couple of burly men in suits and ear pieces standing at one corner, and bet that if he could see through the mass of revelers he'd see a similar pair at the far corner.

Club security.

He bet they were well-trained to spot suspicious characters, so either they were in on it (unlikely since they didn't look like they were going anywhere) or whoever planted the bomb was an employee.

Probably some technician who had reason to go under there with a tool bag.

He strolled over, pretending to stare at the beautiful girls dancing on stage. The security gave him a brief glance and paid him no more attention.

Aaron moved around the platform on the beach side as if he was going to walk around it and continue along the shore. He kept a sharp eye out for anyone suspicious or any gap in the cloth covering the sides of the dance floor. He saw nothing.

Damn it. How the hell am I going to get under there?

He made it to the far side where the bar stood. A crowd of people waited to be served, standing between the bar and the dance floor. While he could probably get under the platform there without security seeing him, the bartenders might spot him and certainly some of the visitors would.

Would they do anything? One thing he'd learned after so many operations is that you could usually discount members of the general public. They hardly reacted to anything.

Usually. In any crowd there might be a loudmouth, someone who would get suspicious of anything strange and immediately call attention to it. It might just be a joke, it might be a complaint, but anything that brought attention to him pulling a stunt like that would bring in security, and then he wouldn't be able to stop the bomb.

Aaron kept making a circuit of the stage. Security paid him no attention. Coming to the side with the DJ booth, he saw the DJ, a young Arab guy, working the records while adding a bass beat and some flair from prerecordings. Aaron had never liked House music or even understood it, but he saw this guy was giving him an opportunity.

Because the platform with all his gear was separate from the dance floor, ringed with its own railing and with a security guard standing right next to it. Apparently, this guy was famous enough to warrant his own guard. In between his platform and the dance floor was a ten-foot stretch of sand filled with dancers, their hands in the air, one guy blowing a whistle in time to the music.

A whole bunch of them were packed in there, enough that neither the DJ or security would notice him slipping under the stage.

But wouldn't the dancers notice?

Maybe not. They were all facing the DJ, and half of them looked drunk or high or both.

Aaron suppressed a negative judgment of the people he was trying to save and got to work. Pretending to get into some music he didn't like, he began moving with the beat and dancing into the crowd. He was way too old to be here and dressed way too badly, but nobody seemed to care.

He danced through the crowd until he ended up at the back, right next to the stage. From his vantage point, the security guard was nothing but a shaved head briefly glimpsed through the upraised arms of the dancers, and the DJ remained focused on his electronics equipment. All the dancers on the sand faced him, their backs to Aaron.

The people on the dance floor were another story. Separated only by a safety railing, Aaron was looking right at their knees, and they looked right down on him. Any of them at the edge of the dance floor could see what he was doing if they bothered to look at him.

No choice but to risk it. The bomb could go off at any moment. Aaron dropped to the ground and rolled under the stage.

He found himself in a forest of metal struts holding up the dance floor. The wood above him thudded with the movements of hundreds of feet. He took off his sunglasses and peered around, waiting for his eyes to adjust from the bright sunlight outside to the shady space beneath the platform.

He crawled forward on the sand, the music sounding muffled, blocked out by the banging of the dance floor just inches above his head. The bomb would probably be set near the center to spread the blast across as much of the dance floor as possible. He made his way in that direction.

It didn't take long to find—a mound of sand dead center below the platform. No need to hide it much if no one's going to look, and even if a technician came down here, they wouldn't think twice about a low hump of sand.

Aaron knew better.

He crawled over to it and carefully wiped the sand off with his hands to reveal a metal dome about the dimensions of a covered turkey platter you'd use on Thanksgiving. Set in its side was a small rectangular shape covered by a plastic bag.

The timer, wrapped in plastic to protect it from the sand.

Aaron pulled an X-ACTO knife from his fanny pack and slit it open.

His eyes went wide when he saw there was only one minute left on the timer.

No sweat. It was a simple model. He just needed to remove the timer's case and snip a single wire.

He pulled out a mini mag light, turned it on, and placed it in his mouth to keep his hands free. Next, he pulled out a tiny Phillips-head screwdriver and started to unscrew the first of four screws holding the front of the case to the back.

The music rose in tempo and volume, and above him, the dancers all started jumping up and down at the same time.

Thump. Thump. Thump.

Just as he got the first screw off, he noticed a sudden brightening of the light around him.

Glancing to his right, he saw a young man in a resort uniform crawling toward him, murder in his eyes.

Crap. In keeping with his beach outfit, Aaron didn't have any weapons.

Thump. Thump. Thump.

Never mind. He didn't need weapons to kill someone. He'd done it with his bare hands plenty of times.

The guy paused and pulled out a knife.

Well, that evens things up a bit.

Aaron checked the timer. Forty seconds. He worked on getting the next screw out as the terrorist crawled for him.

He got it out just before the guy got in striking range.

The terrorist lashed out at him with the knife. Aaron dodged to the side, getting one of the struts between him and the enemy. Another attack. Aaron dodged again, tried to grab the man's knife hand and nearly got cut in the attempt.

Thump. Thump. Thump.

The music and dancing continued, oblivious to the annihilation about to be unleased on the club.

Trying not to think of the time, Aaron crouched behind the thin metal strut, his only protection, and the guy wove back and forth, threatening to attack from either side.

Then a feint, and bob back to the other side, and a lightning fast thrust at Aaron's face.

Aaron's was a fraction of a second quicker. He grabbed the knife arm and twisted until he heard the joint snap, plucked the knife out of the hand the instant it let go of the weapon, and plunged it through the man's other hand.

He didn't want to kill this guy. Not yet.

Aaron dove back to the timer, hoping the guy didn't have enough willpower to try anything with a broken wrist and a skewered hand. You should never underestimate your opponent, but then again, you should never underestimate the power of a time bomb with twenty seconds left before it blows up two feet from your head.

Thump. Thump. Thump.

Twenty seconds. Aaron reached for where he had dropped his screwdriver and found it no longer there.

Desperately searching around, he found it a couple of feet to his left. He must have kicked in accidentally during the fight.

He grabbed it and got the next screw off in record time.

The fourth screw got stuck.

Thump. Thump. Thump.

Cursing through gritted teeth, he yanked on it as hard as he could, heard and felt the plastic case snap, and it came off, revealing the circuitry below and a clock almost run back to a meeting with mortality.

Aaron grabbed his wire cutters and snipped the wire with seconds to spare.

The music reached a crescendo, and the dancers above him let out a cheer. Aaron grinned and saluted them.

Only to get kicked in the side of the head.

The terrorist wasn't out of the game yet. He had managed to pull the knife out of his own hand, the blood around his mouth showing he'd done it with his teeth, and he was even managing to hold it.

Probably not too well, which is why he decided to kick Aaron instead of stab him.

The foot drove forward again, this time at Aaron's groin. Aaron managed to twist just enough to take it on the inside of this thigh, then rolled away, only to get a parting kick in the small of his back.

Now he was up and ready. The terrorist snarled, made a weak swipe that Aaron easily deflected, the knife tumbling out of his bloody grasp, and then Aaron gave him a one-two punch that put him face down in the sand.

Aaron gave a brief strike to the snapped wrist and the perforated hand, the man flailing with pain, then he flipped him over, got him in a choke hold, and tried to pry his mouth open.

Too late. He heard the snap of glass as the Order operative bit down on a cyanide capsule.

Aaron cursed. They always did that when about to be captured. He'd tried to capture a prisoner a dozen times, always with the same result.

The man grinned up at him, the corners of his mouth twitching as the first convulsions set in.

"G-good l-l-luck," the guy said in Arabic.

"Huh?"

"G-g-good luck p-p-protecting your d-d-daughter." His entire body shook and he began to foam at the mouth, his jaw working, blood flecking his lips as he involuntarily ground the glass vial between his teeth. With a final effort, he opened it. "W-we k-know where she is."

His head twitched, his eyes rolled back, and with a final tremor across all his body, went stiff and lifeless.

CHAPTER FOUR

"I don't know how The Sword of the Righteous managed to track us down," Jana said. "We're here on fake CIA passports and we've told no one where we are."

"I don't understand it either," Jacob replied.

They sat in their hotel room, a different one than the one they had been in the previous night, rented not under their false names but with the name of a U.S. embassy worker who was in the loop. That should keep them safe, Jana hoped.

The killer, as both Jana and Jacob had suspected, got away. The police were trying to track him based on CCTV video, but neither held out much hope. He had appeared from nowhere, and would disappear just as readily. The Sword of the Righteous was good at that.

"Let's take a look at that site you mentioned," Jacob said, opening up his computer linked to an encrypted satellite phone. "Wallace has given me blanket access to all satellite imagery for the Middle East."

Tyler Wallace was the CIA station director in Athens and Jacob's direct superior. While Jana had never met him face to face, she felt like she knew him, given how much Jacob talked about him. A good man and an effective one. Jacob had a deep respect for him, and it was not easy to earn Jacob Snow's respect.

"So where was it? Just west of the Libyan/Egyptian border?"

"Yes. Near a village called Al Jaghbub."

"I know it. It's the last in a string of oases stretching west from the Nile. Kind of small, but a good stopover for the smuggling trade."

"Or ancient, more legitimate trade routes," Jana said. "I think the ancient Egyptians must have guarded this oasis as the terminus of their trade with the Libyans. The general consensus is that Siwa was that terminus, but perhaps they pushed even further west."

"I thought you told me the ancient Egyptians and Libyans fought all the time," Jacob said, typing in coordinates.

"When they weren't doing business. That was common in ancient times."

"Not too different today. Ah! Here we are."

A satellite image of a dusty desert town that couldn't have had a population of more than a few thousand appeared on the screen. A patch of green off to one side showed the location of the oasis.

"It was to the northeast," Jana said. "On the top of a hill."

Jacob zoomed out a little and moved the view to the northeast. Jana's expert eyes studied the landscape.

"Zoom out a little more."

Jacob did as he was asked.

"There!" Jana said, pointing. "Zoom in on that hill."

She had spotted a rocky hill with a large top that appeared to be relatively flat. As Jacob zoomed in, she spotted the outline of several buildings, including two large ones, surrounded by a wall.

"A temple and fort inside a protective wall," Jana whispered. "Just like in the Sudan."

Jacob zoomed in a little closer, bringing the hilltop into sharp focus. He moved the view slowly from one side of the hilltop to the other. A large square structure with thick walls was no doubt the fort, and several smaller buildings were scattered around it.

And close to the fort stood the foundations of a stone structure in the classic layout of an Egyptian temple. She could make out the foundations of two pylons in front of the building, then a rectangular temple with a main hall and a smaller altar room in back.

When she looked at that altar room, her heart did a flip-flop.

"Zoom in there," Jana said, pointing.

He zoomed in on the altar room and cursed.

Because while he was no archaeologist, he knew how to interpret satellite photos.

Right at the back of the altar room was the circular shadow of a pit, and inside that was a vague lighter form that might have been the top of the statue.

"They've already been there," Jana gasped. "How old is this image?"

Jacob checked. "Just from this morning. The satellites take photos of sensitive areas every day if they can."

"Do you have access to older photos?"

"One minute."

Jacob typed a few commands and brought up a series of photos of the same region for the past two weeks.

Flipping through them, they soon found that the excavation had to have occurred the day before. All the earlier photos showed undisturbed ground.

"Good," Jacob said.

"Good? They have the Staff of Ra! They can make a nuke."

"Good in the sense that they just got it. We have a chance to intercept them."

"Not much of a chance," Jana grunted. "I'm sure they've completed as much of the bomb as they can and are only waiting for the uranium. Once they have that, it might only be a matter of days or hours."

Jacob gave her a ghoulish grin. "Now you're thinking like a CIA operative."

"Perpetually pessimistic and always assuming the worst-case scenario is the one we're facing?"

"Pretty much, yeah."

Jana stared at the screen for a while, her mind working. She noticed Jacob watching her, but he didn't interrupt. She liked guys who didn't interrupt her when she was thinking.

"You know … " she said at last. "The Sword of the Righteous might not have stolen this Staff of Ra."

"Well somebody did! Look at that hole. It's brand new, and that sure looks like the site in the Sudan."

"It does. There are some differences, but that could be down to terrain and a different level of preservation. A lot more is covered up in the Libyan site. But it's close enough, and the geography fits. So I'm thinking this really is the site we're looking for, but that doesn't mean it was stolen by Dr. Farag and his crew."

"Who the hell else knows about it?"

"Plenty of people now. You told me once that membership in terrorist groups is fluid, with people leaving one organization to join others if they're more successful."

Jacob nodded. "Happened with ISIS. A lot of fighters from smaller groups joined Islamic State when they started doing so well. And The Sword of the Righteous gained a lot of respect for the Suez Canal bombing. People are going to join them, not leave them."

"Maybe. Or maybe that's their way of joining them."

Jacob snapped his fingers. "I see what you're getting at. Now that the word is out that The Sword of the Righteous is looking for certain artifacts, someone in the know might have raided this temple so they can give it to the organization. That would get them membership and a big promotion on day one. Oh, wait. What if someone simply wanted to make money and dug it up to sell it to them? Damn. Our list of suspects just got a whole lot longer."

"Yeah, especially since Dr. Farag is laying low right now. He might have even commissioned someone to get it for him, or made it known that he wanted to purchase it."

Jacob rubbed his chin. "So that might give us a bit more time. The question is, how do we figure out who's got it? Terrorist chatter is at an all-time low. Remember how every major power made a huge sweep a month ago when we thought Dr. Farag already had a nuke? The U.S., Britain, France, Egypt, and a bunch of other states rounded up every terror cell they could and to hell with the evidence. It was the biggest crackdown since 9/11. That's got them all being really careful. We may have taken out a ton of terrorists, but now it's ten times harder finding out what the remaining ones are up to."

"So we don't go after the terrorists," Jana said.

"Huh?"

"I mean, obviously, we continue to try and track down Dr. Farag. That's the number one priority. He's got ten kilos of fissile material from the Karnak staff, after all. But we should also investigate the illegal antiquities market. If it was stolen by someone else, someone who wants to sell it to The Sword of the Righteous, that's going to make ripples in the black market. Your average antiquities dealer isn't going to know how to get in contact with such an organization, especially now that the authorities are hounding them all over the globe."

"So we come at them from a different angle," Jacob said, nodding in appreciation. "Nice."

Jana blushed and grinned. His approval meant a lot to her. Strange, considering how a few months ago, she wanted nothing to do with him or his lifestyle. Funny how things changed.

Saving the world has become addictive.

"So how do we start?" Jana asked. "I've always been on the legal side of archaeology."

Jacob pulled out his phone. "I know just the place. But first, we need to book seats on the next flight to Palermo. One of the main smuggling routes from Libya and Egypt goes through Sicily, and I have a good contact there who knows everything that moves through there. So pack your bags. We're going to Italy."

Jana burst out laughing.

Jacob looked up. "What?"

"When I was studying in the library, I was thinking you'd like Italy better than France, and now you're suggesting we go to Sicily."

"So, were you thinking this before or after you saved my life with a book?"

"Pretty good timing on shoving that book into his line of sight, eh? Although I got to admit it was pure luck."

"Not pure luck. Quick thinking. Plus some luck." His face darkened. "And we're going to need a lot more luck where we're going. This won't be a pleasure trip."

"It never is with you," Jana said and laughed.

Jacob looked hurt. "Sorry."

"Oh! I mean … It's just that we've been caught up in all this craziness. It's not your fault."

Jacob grimaced. "It is, though. I first reached out to you because you had information I needed. I took you out of that excavation where you had made the biggest discovery of your career and turned your world upside down. I screwed up your life."

Jana stood and walked over to him, putting a hand on his cheek. "No, the terrorists screwed up my life, and they'll screw it up a whole lot more if they get a chance. I don't regret meeting you, Jacob. Not one little bit. You've given me a whole new life. And the biggest discovery of my career? That Roman mosaic? Yeah, like that can compare to a secret network of tunnels under the Dome of the Rock or a perfectly preserved pirate ship."

Jacob hung his head.

"Both of which got blown up," he mumbled.

"Again, not your fault. You … we … are just trying to reduce the amount of damage the bad guys are doing. Yes, part of those ancient Israelite tunnels got blown up, but imagine what would have happened if the terrorists had won? It would have all been destroyed. And those modern-day pirates would have found the ship if we hadn't, and released the bioweapon, killing thousands if not hundreds of thousands of innocent Mexicans and tourists. We actually *prevented* destruction. It's terrible that some historical artifacts got ruined in the process, but that's not on us."

"It's on me that you got dragged into this in the first place."

"I'm not sorry."

Jacob blinked, staring at her.

"When did that change?"

Jana looked away, giving a little shrug. She had always resented Jacob for taking up so much time with her father, and then hated him more when her father supposedly got killed in action. After that, she hadn't spoken to anyone at the CIA, Jacob included. She wanted nothing to do with that life ever again.

And when Jacob showed up at her dig site in Morocco, looking for information for one of his missions, she wanted to slap him more than cooperate. And she had hated being stuck with him on subsequent missions. She resented being taken away from her career, was terrified of the danger, disgusted by the lengths the terrorists would go to cause havoc and bloodshed, and perpetually annoyed by Jacob's arrogant, infantile behavior.

And yet, she had grown to love it. Well, not love it, more like be addicted to it. The adventure, the importance of what they were doing, had gotten under her skin. That had made her understand Jacob, and her father, a whole lot better.

So what about Jacob's question? When did it exactly change for her?

"I don't know when that changed," Jana admitted. "It's been changing bit by bit for a while. Remember how I kept sneaking along to help? At first I didn't want to. I did it because I felt I had to. At some point, my sense of duty and my wants melded."

"The CIA isn't even trying to keep you out of the loop anymore," Jacob said. "You've been too useful."

"Maybe I can be useful in Palermo. Remember that trick we pulled on that Spanish collector? Maybe we might end up repeating that operation."

"You mean the operation where I nearly got ripped apart by dogs? Yeah, that was a raging success."

"It was, although a bit messy."

"Messy is my middle name. Let's get that plane to Palermo. But I got to warn you, we'll have a lot more to contend with there than a few dogs. These guys play for high stakes, and they don't like intruders."

"What about the people chasing us? They obviously know our aliases. If we book a flight, they'll simply follow us to Sicily."

Jacob grinned, went over to his suitcase, and opened a hidden pocket. Jana jerked in surprise. As his hands went for it, she hadn't seen an opening on the suitcase's black fabric, and yet suddenly there was one. Even watching him directly, she hadn't seen how he opened it. He pulled out a pair of Canadian passports and held them up.

"One for you and one for me."

"The CIA is generous."

Jacob's face darkened. "These aren't from the CIA."

"What?"

"I bought them on the black market. Swiped one of your passport photos from your purse. Sorry."

"Why are you buying passports on the black market?"

Jacob's face darkened further. "Because there might be a leak in the CIA. Or maybe more than one, and they're high up."

CHAPTER FIVE

As Jacob entered the famous medieval Capella Palatina in Sicily, he looked around nervously, checking every corner, every column for hidden threats. He scanned the crowd too—various tourists alone or in small groups, plus a Chinese tour group being led by an Italian woman speaking remarkably good Mandarin. While Jacob spoke fluent Arabic, Spanish, and a smattering of other languages, he'd always been impressed by people able to get their tongue around the Far Eastern languages with their complex and subtle tonal systems.

The church was even more impressive. A large chapel was framed by soaring arches on each side, their surfaces covered with golden mosaics on which were depicted Christ and all the saints in rich blues, browns, and reds. In the half dome above the altar, a beautifully rendered Jesus held up the Bible with one hand and blessed the congregation with the other.

Jana had told him this chapel was built by the Normans in the 12th century, using Byzantine artisans to make its famous mosaic. He spotted an Islamic influence as well in the style of the arches, which looked like arches he'd seen in mosques and religious schools in Morocco.

While he didn't know much about history, Sicily had always been a center for trade, with a mixture of different cultures interacting or fighting. It seemed it had been no different in medieval times.

He wished Jana was by his side explaining all this stuff to him, but he wasn't here as a tourist like he was pretending, and Jana was on the other side of the chapel, pretending to take pictures of the mosaics but really keeping watch.

Jacob had arranged to meet an old informant of his, Francesca Miceli. While the various smugglers who used Sicily as a way station traded in migrants or drugs or weapons, Francesca Miceli traded in information. If an illegal shipment passed through Sicily, she knew about it. And if she knew about it, she'd tell you about it for the right price.

How she got her information, Jacob didn't know. How she survived informing on criminals for a living seemed to him a miracle. Maybe all these angels and saints looked over her. She was a devout Catholic, after all.

And there she was now, coming into the chapel. Dressed in a designer outfit, she looked like a successful businesswoman in her early forties, although she was far more interesting than that. She stopped at the basin next to the door, touched her finger to the water, then bent her knee and crossed herself. Jacob took a seat in one of the pews. Jana had gone out of sight. Good.

He spotted a sharp-eyed Italian man in a nice suit shadowing Francesca. A bodyguard, and a skilled one by the looks of him. Fair enough. Francesca always had a bodyguard with her, although come to think of it Jacob had never seen the same bodyguard twice.

Did she have a whole host of bodyguards, or did they just keep getting killed? Jacob couldn't say. What Jacob knew about Francesca Miceli was far outweighed by what he didn't know.

The important thing was that her intel was always reliable. He did know that. Every time he'd come to her for information, he got what he wanted.

And they had always met here. He had to hand it to Italian criminals. They may do horrible things, but they always did them in the most beautiful places.

Francesca moved to the pew he sat at and took a place an arm's length from him. No other worshippers were nearby, although a steady trickle of tourists walked past. The informant crossed herself again, clasped her hands in prayer, and bowed her head.

Jacob kept quiet. This was not an act.

Once she was done praying for forgiveness for what must have been an epic list of sins, she spoke quietly, not looking away from the image of Christ above the altar.

"How can I help you, Mr. Briggs?"

John Briggs. Another of his aliases and the one that Francesca Miceli knew him by.

"Any big shipments come through in the past couple of days?"

He set his jacket down on the seat between them, with a pile of cash beneath it. The informant didn't reach for it at once. Subtlety kept her alive.

"A couple. Anything in particular you're looking for?"

"Antiquities or armaments."

"No. Nothing like that. With the situation in North Africa, shipments have all but dried up."

Jacob nodded. A lot of warships in the Mediterranean these days. It had put a crimp into all sorts of smuggling operations.

"Any news of a shipment coming in?"

"None."

Her hand eased down beneath his jacket and withdrew so quickly that if he hadn't been expecting the movement, Jacob would have never seen it. Even looking, he didn't see her palm the wad of bills he'd put beneath the jacket and didn't see where she secreted it.

I wonder if she got her start as a pickpocket?

"I do have some news, though," she said.

"What's that?"

"It's big news. Very hush hush. It has to do with a major auction of an artifact. It came from the region you're interested in, but the auction isn't happening in Sicily."

An auction? That didn't fit. But how many major artifacts could suddenly go on sale right now?

"Tell me more."

"Gladly."

Silence.

Francesca stared at the image of Christ, not saying anything.

Jacob suppressed his irritation and slipped another wad of bills beneath his jacket. This time, he didn't even see her remove it, although he had no doubt that she did. The only thing more reliable than Francesca Miceli's accuracy was her greed.

"It's happening in three days' time. In Gibraltar. It's being run by George Dawson."

"Who?"

"He's *the* major player in the sale of Nazi memorabilia. Such items are illegal in many nations, and so they can fetch a high price."

"I'm not looking for Nazi artifacts."

"This isn't, although there's a Nazi connection. Have you heard of Rommel's treasure?"

"Erwin Rommel, the Afrika Korps general?"

"Yes. When he conquered most of North Africa during World War Two, he closed in on Egypt, and came very close to taking it."

"I know that. I don't know about any treasure."

"As he moved across North Africa, members of the Gestapo attached to his army looted valuables from any Jewish families they came across. North Africa had many Jews back then."

Jacob nodded. In Tangier and Asilah, he had been to beautiful synagogues built centuries ago, testament to once-thriving communities. Many Jews had moved to Israel after it was founded in 1948, and many more left in the 50s and 60s as one by one, Morocco, Tunisia, Libya, and Algeria gained their independence. That soon after World War Two, the Jews rightly worried about new pogroms. They feared these newly independent nations might turn on their native Jewish populations.

The informant went on.

"That wasn't the only thing they collected. As you probably know, many high-ranking Nazi officials were fascinated by the occult, especially the forgotten powers and knowledge of ancient civilizations. They were eagerly anticipating the conquest of British Egypt, not only to control the Suez Canal, but also to find ancient artifacts there. Rumor has it, they found some important ancient Egyptian artifact at an isolated oasis on the Libyan-Egyptian border."

Jacob shifted in his seat, confused. That sounded like a dead ringer for what they were looking for, right down to the location, but if it was dug up in the early 1940s, what did the terrorists just dig up a couple of days ago?

Or did they dig and find nothing?

"What kind of artifact is it?"

"It's Egyptian, but the description is vague. Dawson put out an announcement that he was taking bidders, and only said that it was for a 'withering power.' I have no idea what that means. It must be code for people in the know."

Jacob tensed. The 'withering power of Ra' was what the ancients called the Staff of Ra, capable of firing a beam of radiation at the enemy with fearful results. Dr. Farag and the rest of The Sword of the Righteous knew this.

Did anyone else?

So it hadn't been their old nemesis who dug up the site in Libya. This guy in Gibraltar beat them to it, or maybe Rommel beat them both to it.

And he obviously wasn't in The Sword of the Righteous if he was putting the staff up for auction. He knew they wanted it, though, and apparently he knew of others who wanted it too.

Great. More people in the mix. That just made their lives a whole lot harder.

"So can anyone go to this auction?"

"Yes. It takes place at Dawson's house this Wednesday evening. You have access to the Dark Web?"

"Yes."

You wouldn't believe the things I've dug into in that online cesspool. Then again, maybe you would.

"Look for a site called Third Reich Mementoes. That's Dawson's. It will give you the exact time and address. You'll need to apply to go, though. It's not an open house."

"Apply to go?"

"Like any other private auction for high-ticket items. You need to prove you're both interested and have the funds to cover your bid."

Jacob nodded, an idea forming in his mind.

"Anything else I can help you with?" Francesca Miceli asked.

"What kind of man is this George Dawson character?"

"I don't know. I've never dealt with him. I hope this information proves useful to you."

She stood, crossed herself as she gazed up at the mosaic of Jesus, then turned and left the chapel. Her bodyguard followed her out, as close and quiet as a shadow.

Jacob lingered for a minute, then got up too. Out of the corner of his eye, he spotted Jana moving toward him. Without looking at her, he left the building, crossed the plaza out front, and started walking down a side street.

Jana moved in beside him.

"Find out anything useful?" she asked.

"I found out that dinner you planned for us is going to be our only one in Italy. We need to go to Greece."

"Greece? Why?"

"Two reasons. First, there's a contact I have in Athens who is going to prove useful for the next phase of this operation, and also we need a place to hide. I don't trust our passports to stay clean for long. Someone's watching us, and they're watching us closely."

"If they're compromised, the terrorists will know if we fly to Athens."

"Yes, but they won't know where we're staying. We won't check into a hotel. We'll go to my house. No one knows where my house is except a few people in the CIA."

"I don't understand how they could have found out the names and numbers of those CIA passports."

"I'm trying to figure that out myself."

It did seem unlikely that a terrorist organization that was in hiding and on the run would be able to find out about some passports the CIA had only given them a few weeks ago. That made him worried.

Worried that it hadn't been the terrorists who discovered their new aliases.

Because a few weeks before, Aaron Peters, Jana's father, had taken him aside and spoken to him alone.

Spoken to him about The Order, an ultrasecret organization that pulled the strings behind many corporations, governments and terror groups, and who might even be pulling the strings behind The Sword of the Righteous.

Aaron had warned him that The Order had spread its tentacles into all the major intelligence organizations. His mentor thought that even the CIA itself was compromised.

At first, Jacob hadn't wanted to believe it. Now, it was looking like that was possible.

CHAPTER SIX

When Jacob heard "collector of Nazi memorabilia", he could think of only one person.

Vasiliki Castellanos.

Based in Athens, this multi-millionaire owned numerous freighters that plied the Mediterranean and Atlantic on short to mid-length runs. Much of his traffic was between the North and West African coasts and Europe. This gave Castellanos the perfect opportunity to dabble in smuggling—of drugs and of people—to pad out his profits. He then sold his imports to dealers in Europe. He didn't do the dirty work of selling the goods himself.

No, Vasiliki Castellanos was a respectable businessman. Everyone said so, from the politicians he bribed to the museums in Athens that he generously donated to and the common people in the little village he was born in who he helped get through Greece's grinding economic crisis.

"Open-handed Vasiliki." That's what the press called him.

Jacob knew better.

The reason Jacob had thought of him was for two reasons.

One, he wasn't above taking bribes from the CIA to provide useful information.

And two, he was well-known to have one of the largest collections of World War Two memorabilia in Europe. The man's house was literally a museum. Every now and then, he opened it up to journalists and gave them a tour. Jacob had watched one of these tours on Greek TV and wondered what drove a man to have an entire parking garage full of old tanks, trucks, and armored cars.

I guess everyone needs a hobby, he thought as he drove his Camaro up to the gated community in the hills overlooking Athens.

Jana was not with him. He had left her at his house, delving into the Dark Web to find out what she could about George Dawson and his auction in Gibraltar.

The guard at the gate took his name—another false one—and waved him through. Jacob had had dealings with Vasiliki Castellanos before, and when he got in touch, the multimillionaire had told him to come right over.

Jacob drove slowly along the narrow residential roads past gaudy mansions that showed more money than taste. Greece had never fully recovered from the financial crisis of 2009, and many people lived hand to mouth in squalid apartments. To see such ostentatious wealth so close to all that suffering irritated him. It reminded him too much of the Third World.

At the very top of the slope, he came to another gate, this one operated electronically. To either side stood sentry boxes with mannequins standing in them. One was of an American GI from World War Two. Another was a soldier from the Greek army from that same conflict. Both were dressed in what he assumed were vintage uniforms with all the equipment, right down to the rifles.

Jacob pushed the intercom button, identified himself, and the gate clicked open.

He drove up a sweeping driveway toward the gleaming white mansion on top of the hill, noting the security cameras and advanced alarm system.

The garage was shut, so he parked in front of the steps leading up to the front door.

Vasiliki Castellanos emerged, a stout Greek man in his late middle age with thick arms and a thicker middle. He gripped two large German Shepherds at the end of a pair of chains.

Jacob remembered infiltrating the home of a Spanish collector and getting chased by a pair of enormous Dobermans.

What is it with rich collectors and vicious dogs? I hope I don't get my ass bitten like last time.

"Mr. Thompson," Castellanos greeted him. "How nice to see you again."

"Thank you for meeting me at your home."

"I wanted you to see it. We've done enough business that it's about time I showed you around my sanctum sanctorum."

Jacob didn't know what that meant. Maybe he should have brought along Jana after all.

"I'd be interested in seeing it."

Military museums were the only kind of museums he actually liked visiting. Not that he would tell Jana that.

He eyed the German Shepherds. They stared back at him, licking their chops.

Castellanos noticed him looking. "Oh, don't worry about Adolf and Benito. They're a pair of big babies."

Big babies that could rip my throat out if you ordered them to. I know a four-legged bodyguard when I see one, buddy.

Unfortunately, I'm seeing two.

"I have a few questions about an upcoming auction," Jacob said. "The usual deal for information."

The multimillionaire smiled. "The usual deal" was a wad of cash, always welcome but essentially symbolic for someone like him, and also a get-out-of-jail-free card. The CIA would use its influence to keep him safe. While Castellanos trafficked in drugs and migrants, he did not traffic in arms despite his obsession with military history. And he was a good source of intel on who was trafficking arms. The CIA had decided that he was more useful as a free man than in the jail cell he so richly deserved. It was one of those little compromises for the greater good that had never sat well with Jacob, even though he understood the logic behind it.

"We'll sit and have some wine and discuss it," the millionaire said. "But first, let me show you my collection. I think a man like you would appreciate it."

That offhand comment unsettled Jacob a bit. Vasiliki Castellanos should have no idea what kind of man he was. He didn't even know Jacob's real name.

But lately, a lot of people knew a lot more about him than he felt comfortable with.

The Greek descended the steps, his two German Shepherds following obediently, and led Jacob around to a large garage with a higher roof than was normal.

Castellanos clicked a remote, and all five bay doors rose in tandem to reveal an array of tanks.

"Panzer IV, Tiger, Sherman, Challenger, Char B1," Jacob recited, going from left to right.

"They are indeed," Castellanos said, giving him a nod of approval.

"I'm surprised you have a Char B1," Jacob said, pointing to the French tank. It had a large chassis and an undersized, globular turret with a short gun.

"They were never numerous," the collector said. "A pity. With their heavy armor and firepower, they outmatched everything the Germans fielded in the invasion of France. If the French had more of them, the war might have gone differently."

"That and better communication."

The Germans had equipped every tank with its own radio to coordinate maneuvers while the French still relied on waving pennants in order to signal each other, an ineffective and dangerous system.

"Yes, knowledge is power," Castellanos said.

You're telling me.

Vasiliki Castellanos led him into the garage, and Jacob saw it went back a lot further than he had thought. Beyond he saw halftracks, trucks, motorcycles, and armored cars from every European power. Along the wall were display cases containing everything from pistols to machine guns to grenades.

They walked slowly around the exhibition space, discussing the various items. Castellanos turned out to be an amiable and knowledgeable host, and Jacob had to remind himself that the Greek made as much of a living importing hash, MDMA, and illegal immigrants as he did the legal cargo in his freighters.

"You sure have an impressive collection," Jacob said in all truth. Then he decided to probe. "I notice that while you have some German gear, you don't have any SS stuff or swastika flags, just material from the Wehrmacht."

Castellanos clicked his tongue. "I don't want such things. I'm an historian and collector, not a Nazi lover."

"Good to hear. I've seen collections that were almost all Nazi paraphernalia."

"The Nazis were evil. They did terrible things to Greece because we stood up to them. Our partisan groups were some of the best in the war, and the Nazis made us suffer for it."

"People starved."

"My own grandparents starved. I had a great uncle I never met because he died of rickets during those days. A trip to the hospital could have cured him. Even a trip to a well-stocked grocery store could have cured him. But there were no hospitals and no well-stocked grocery stores for Greeks during the occupation. Come, let's have some of that wine. I have a nice Assyrtiko from 1984. Do you know it?"

"Santorini produces some of the best wine in Greece."

"That it does, my friend, that it does."

Castellanos brought him into a spacious living room where a young Chinese man with a shaved head was setting out wine glasses and a bowl of olives on a small table between two antique leather armchairs.

While the servant's loose white clothing hid his muscles, his grace and economy of movement told Jacob that he was a trained martial artist.

The thick callouses on his knuckles was another sign, as was the way his hand muscles bulged as he uncorked the bottle, poured two generous glasses, and left the room on silent silk slippers.

Vasiliki Castellanos sat, his dogs flanking him, eyes on Jacob.

He raised his glass. "To history."

"To history," Jacob repeated, raising his own.

They drank. The millionaire looked at him expectantly.

"So you don't like people who buy and sell Nazi memorabilia," Jacob said.

"No, I do not."

"Then you probably don't like George Dawson of Gibraltar."

Castellanos's brow furrowed. "If I was still a boy living in my village, I would spit on the floor at the mention of his name. Now I am a bit more acquainted with the social graces."

"He has a big auction coming up."

"Ah yes, the 'withering power.' Do you know what that means?"

"No."

"Neither do I, if that's the information you're looking for."

"Do you know anything about the item in question?" Jacob asked.

"All I know is that it is an Egyptian artifact collected by Rommel's army during World War Two. Part of the famous Rommel's treasure so many hack documentaries have spun so many fairy tales about."

Now Jacob really wished he had brought Jana along. He hadn't even heard of Rommel's treasure. But he had left her in his private residence on the coast just east of Athens to keep her safe. Whoever attacked her in Paris might still be tracking them, and being in his house, which was not only a top secret location but built like a fort, would keep her out of danger.

Because even after all the adventures they'd been on, and all the brushes with death she had faced without flinching, Jacob Snow still wanted to protect her.

"So what's the real story?" Jacob asked.

"Throughout the North African campaign, Rommel was constantly outgunned and undersupplied. Hitler had overstretched his nation when he invaded Russia, so Rommel was perpetually starved of tanks, men, petrol, and everything else necessary to continue the campaign. It's a testament to his abilities as a general that he lasted in North Africa as long as he did. So as the fortunes of war turned against him in late 1942 and he found himself defending a smaller and smaller patch of the region, he was given orders to get his collection of antiquities out before the inevitable fall. I believe it was Goebbels who gave the order. Hitler could never admit a campaign was going badly, and Goebbels, although fanatically loyal to the Führer, was more pragmatic.

"It was the Italian navy that was responsible for Axis shipping during the North African campaign, so the treasure was packed up and sent to Italy. According to some Italian documents circulating after the war, they were initially kept in a cave outside Rome, where they would be safe from bombing. After that, the trail goes cold. The treasure was never recovered, and there is no record of what happened to it after the end of 1942."

"But the war had another two-and-a-half years to go," Jacob said.

"Indeed. Many records were destroyed during those final years, of course."

"But there must have been eyewitnesses. Rumors."

"A plethora of both. None of them reliable. Rommel's treasure took on the status of a myth, although it was quite real, at least for a time. Perhaps the gold and jewelry stolen from the Jews was liquidated to fund the war effort. The antiquities seem to have vanished. Now Dawson has claimed to have recovered at least one of them."

The most important one.

Looks like we're going to Gibraltar.

"I have another favor to ask."

Castellanos didn't reply. Jacob went on.

"I need a reason to get into Dawson's house. I and a companion need to pose as potential buyers, but Dawson will ask for proof of legitimacy."

"I cannot vouch for you, firstly because our connection is secret and I wish it to remain so, but also because my hatred of Nazi memorabilia is well known. I wouldn't aid anyone in getting into that auction. But I do have a colleague who owes me a favor. He can vouch for you, and the favor he owes me will be transferred to you."

Jacob shifted in his seat. He didn't like the millionaire's tone.

"And what will that cost me?"

Vasiliki Castellanos smiled. "I will collect the favor at some future time. I know you will honor your debt because I have been of continuing use to your organization."

Jacob nodded his agreement. He was going beyond his authority to put the CIA in debt to this crook, but it was the only way forward.

The bosses back in the States could chew him out later. His main concern was getting into that auction without Dawson's bodyguard gunning him down.

CHAPTER SEVEN

Jana curled her lip in disgust and stared at her screen. She sat in the living room of Jacob's gorgeous living room, which had floor-to-ceiling windows overlooking a rugged, rocky coastline and an azure sea. The house was modern and well-appointed, and Jacob had informed her the glass was bulletproof and the walls made of thick reinforced concrete.

She felt safe for the moment, but what she saw on her computer disturbed her.

Jacob had hooked her up to the Dark Web, a place into which she had never had a reason to venture. Since the Dark Web isn't searchable, he brought up several lists of websites for her to look through in order to find Third Reich Mementoes and any related sites.

And then he had left her to go meet that millionaire smuggler. She had wanted to go with him, but time was of the essence and she was better off here, doing background research.

And what research! While she knew that trading in Nazi memorabilia was popular in some circles, she'd never actually delved into it. The lists Jacob had brought up for her linked to several sites offering such items, along with sites offering guns, drugs, fake IDs, and things she didn't even want to think about and certainly would never click on.

She soon found Third Reich Mementoes and clicked on it, hoping it didn't take her to some nastier site or infect Jacob's laptop with viruses. She supposed the CIA had some pretty good antiviral software, but this was the Dark Web.

The website came up, the title in Gothic lettering flanked by swastikas. A link titled "equip yourself, Aryan!" brought her to a list of mementoes from the Second World War, everything from old Lugers to medals and even a complete set of musical instruments for a Nazi marching band. The trumpets had Nazi flag banners hanging from them, and the drum had a death's head emblazoned on it.

She kept scrolling, shaking her head with a mixture of amazement and disgust as she saw empty cans of Zyklon B, original pamphlets on race ideology, and uniforms supposedly owned by such figures as

Martin Bormann and Hermann Goering. The prices on some of these were eye-popping.

"What would you do if you were a millionaire, Jana?" she whispered. "Any time people asked me that, I said I'd quit teaching and dig full time. Never occurred to me to gather a giant collection of Third Reich garbage."

At the bottom she came to another link labelled, "Auctions for true collectors." She clicked on it.

Three items were up for auction—a letter from 1932 signed by Adolph Hitler to the Gauleiter of the Nazi Party in Dusseldorf, a bloodstained concentration camp uniform with the pink triangle denoting a homosexual prisoner, and a banner proclaiming, "Our rarest item yet. The withering power! If you know, you know. Auction in person only. Must be vetted."

Unlike the other two items, this didn't come with a photo. Bids for the letter and the uniform could be made remotely. Anyone wanting the Libyan Staff of Ra, if indeed Jana's assumption was correct, had to make the journey to Gibraltar.

There was really nothing else of use on the website. Dawson was playing it coy. Not surprising, considering what he had a hold of.

She remembered scrolling past a link to a bulletin board for collectors of Nazi memorabilia. Jana decided to hold her nose and delve into that.

It didn't take her long to find something. One of the most recent threads was labeled "Staff of Ra found?"

Jana nearly had a heart attack when she read those words. What she thought was a little-known conspiracy theory was in fact known to lots of people. She had delved into similar discussion groups on the regular web and found virtually nothing except some off-base rantings by fringe individuals. This thread had 67 comments by more than a dozen usernames.

Since these were all Third Reich nerds, they looked at Dawson's website like some people look at porn.

And they all knew what "the withering power" meant.

The thread started with a link to a website for Sudanese news in English, which gave a brief account of the terrorist attack on Ibn Balamon. While many news outlets had covered the attack, they had all taken the government line that a group of terrorists, perhaps associated with The Sword of the Righteous, had targeted the Christian community in this northern Sudanese town and were repulsed by local security forces. No mention had been made of her and Jacob's involvement or that of the French Foreign Legion.

This site followed the same line, but added the detail that the terrorists had conducted some "illegal diggings" in the adjacent archaeological site, and that "unknown antiquities were robbed from the Sudanese people."

They must have had a reporter on the ground, and some locals told them about our fight in the temple. Then they saw the hole Dr. Farag dug and put two and two together.

The post stated, "It's long been supposed that the Staff of Ra is located on the old Egyptian frontier in northern Sudan. Could the terrorists have been looking for it, using their attack as cover?"

Jana gasped at how close this Internet detective had come to the truth. She wondered who he or she might be.

The rest of the thread was less on target, with everything from conspiracy theories involving Freemasons (backed up by "proof" via numerology) to suggestions that it was all a false flag operation so the Zionists could take over the country. Some of the users got into a flame war about what the Staff of Ra was, the majority coming down on the side of alien technology (from the same aliens who built the pyramids, she supposed) while others contended it was pure magic.

It would have all been laughable except for that one user who started the thread being so close to the truth, as well as a couple of other users who avoided the flame war and concentrated on the reasons why there had been an illegal excavation at the same time as the attack.

"It's obvious The Sword of the Righteous is now in possession of the Staff of Ra."

"Ugh," Jana groaned. "I hope not too many people see this."

A couple of other users claimed the Staff of Ra wasn't there at all, and went at length into their own pet theories.

They were in the minority. The damage had been done, and some anonymous sleuths on the Internet had come perilously close to the truth.

The front door unlocking, followed by the *beep beep beep beep* of a code being punched into the alarm, told her Jacob was home. She turned as footsteps approached the living room.

"You wouldn't believe what I—who the hell are you?"

An older black man in casual civilian clothes strolled into the room and stopped short, staring at her with surprise equal to her own.

Jana sprang to her feet, casting around for the nearest weapon and seeing none. How the hell could a killing machine like Jacob Snow not have a minor arsenal lying around his living room?

"Jana Peters," the man said. He had an American accent.

Jana's hands balled into fists. "Don't come any closer. How the hell did you find me?"

The man shrugged. "I didn't. I suppose you've never seen a photo of me. We've talked on the phone, though."

Jana cocked her head. Now that she thought of it, his voice did sound familiar.

"Tyler Wallace?" she asked.

He smiled. "The same. Where's Jacob?"

"Do you often come into Jacob's house without knocking?"

"I didn't think he'd be here. I wasn't even sure if he was in Greece. You two went dark a couple of days ago. Our agents in Paris couldn't locate you. When I came inside, I heard you and thought you were Jacob."

"How do I know you're Tyler Wallace?" Jana asked, still suspicious.

"I'm going to reach into my pocket. Don't be startled."

Slowly he reached inside his jacket. Jana tensed. He brought out a wallet and opened it up to an American driver's license saying he was Tyler Wallace.

"You show that as proof to a woman who has more passports than pairs of shoes?"

Wallace—if he was Wallace—laughed.

"He's rubbing off on you."

OK, maybe this really was Wallace.

She needed to make sure, though.

"Where did I call you from?" she asked.

"Balochistan."

"Were you happy to hear from me?"

"No. You weren't supposed to be there."

Jana relaxed a bit. Wallace picked up on it, smiled, and pulled a gun from his pocket.

Jana leapt behind the sofa.

"Damn! He really is rubbing off on you. I was giving this to you to make you feel better."

He lobbed the gun over the sofa to land with a thunk on the carpet next to her.

"Never hide behind furniture," he told her. "It's usually not bulletproof."

"This stuff is," Jana said. "He told me."

She picked up the pistol, a 9mm automatic like Jacob favored, checked the magazine and flicked off the safety.

Jana stood, not pointing the gun at him or putting her finger inside the trigger guard but remaining at the ready.

"Feel better?" Wallace asked.

"Yes. I'm almost convinced you are who you say you are."

Wallace sat. "Where is he?"

"Why are you here?"

The older man cocked his head. "Something's got you awful spooked."

"A man tried to assassinate me in the national library in Paris."

"Why didn't Jacob tell me?"

Jana hesitated before answering. "He thinks there might be a leak somewhere."

"A leak? In the CIA?"

Jana only nodded.

"Ridiculous. The Sword of the Righteous followed you somehow. They know your name and know what you look like. Your picture is online."

Jana remembered how a Moroccan news site interviewed her after her discovery of the Roman mosaic. The article had included a photo of her. She had been proud of that, never realizing that it might kill her.

Tyler Wallace went on. "You can't just go dark like that. We haven't heard from you in two days. You haven't used your passports. How did you get back here?"

Jana blushed. "Using some passports, Jacob bought on the black market."

Tyler threw up his hands. "Jesus! He can't do that. He can't use CIA funds to buy something like that without permission and then just vanish off the face of the Earth."

"I'm sorry."

"You're not the one who should apologize. You're a civilian. He knows better. Where is he now?"

"Seeing a contact who might have some information about The Sword of the Righteous. He didn't tell me the details."

Actually, he had told Jana exactly where he was going and why. She felt bad about stretching the truth to Wallace, but she was still not a hundred percent on this conversation. He was sure right about one thing: Jacob had rubbed off on her. At least his paranoia had.

Tyler's gaze flicked over the laptop nearby.

"What the hell? An auction for a Hitler letter and a concentration camp uniform?"

He moved over to take another look. Jana opened her mouth to object and closed it when she couldn't think of what to say.

"Wait, 'the withering power'? Is this about the Staff of Ra?"

Before Jana could answer, an alarm went off. It was a quiet one, certainly not audible outside the house's thick walls, but it carried an odd tonal quality that demanded attention.

Tyler Wallace cursed under his breath and ran over to a screen on the wall. It had already lit up with a view of the outside. Jana rushed to join him.

The monitor, which relayed the images from several cameras, showed half a dozen men in black and wearing balaclavas creeping across the front lawn. Other cameras showed a similar number coming from both sides. A camera at the bottom of the sea cliff showed a pair of men guarding that side, although it didn't offer much of an escape route.

All the men carried automatics. Jana and Tyler were entirely cut off.

Tyler hit a button, and the alarm turned off.

"What do we do?" Jana asked. "This house is totally isolated. No one's going to spot them and call the police."

"We got a minute. See how they're searching the ground? They're trying to find the alarm and don't realize they've already tripped it. They'll figure it out soon, though. We got to arm ourselves."

"All we have is this pistol."

"No, we don't."

Wallace ran into the bedroom.

Despite the situation, she felt embarrassed at the fact that her clothes were in there too.

It didn't matter. Tyler was looking at the viewing screen in the bedroom that had lit up when the alarm went off. The intruders were close to the house now, moving faster and having apparently realized that they had already tripped the alarm.

"I haven't seen any guns in here," Jana said, looking under the bed.

Tyler didn't reply. He simply ran to a blank wall, pressed a spot that looked no different than any other, and a panel slid open.

Inside was a rack of guns and boxes of ammo.

Tyler grinned. “Aw, he left me an M16. He knows I like the classics.”

He grabbed it and stuffed a couple of spare magazines in his pockets. Jana handed back his pistol, which he put in his shoulder holster, and then busied herself with grabbing a Heckler and Koch MP5. This was one of Jacob's favorite weapons, good for close-quarters combat in urban environments. She wasn't an expert at it or any other weapon, but she was a decent shot, and she hoped the rate of fire would help offset any inaccuracy on her part.

As she put a couple of magazines into her pockets, Tyler gestured at three boxes of grenades.

“Frags, stun, smoke,” he said, pointing to each in turn. “Better let me handle these.”

Jana grabbed one of each before she ran out of pocket space. “I’ve used them before.”

“Of course you have. You hang out with Jacob too much.”

Tyler and Jana glanced at the viewing screen in the bedroom.

The front group was running away from the house.

“Oh, crap!” Tyler shouted.

He grabbed her and threw her and himself on the floor.

A moment later, the house was rocked with an explosion, followed by a loud clang. Smoke filled the front hallway just beyond the bedroom door.

CHAPTER EIGHT

Before Jana had recovered from the shockwave, Tyler launched himself up, pulling out a frag grenade as he got to the bedroom door and then tossed it into the front hall.

He ducked back a moment later. The grenade went off, and he gestured to her.

"We got to get out of this bedroom. It's a dead end."

He rushed into the front hall, Jana a step behind him. To the right was an office and a bathroom. Through the open office door, she could see a man fixing what looked like plastic explosives to the window.

Tyler ran to the front door of thick steel, which now lay on the floor, and started firing out. Jana took the opportunity to dart across the open doorway. She had a fleeting glimpse of a couple of figures but nothing more.

Once in position, Jana peeked around the doorway and fired at the first target that presented itself, a guy who was prone behind an olive tree. She didn't hit him, but the long burst chewed up the bark and ground all around him and stopped his fire long enough for Tyler to get to her side of the doorway.

She shouted to him over the gunfire. "They're setting explosives in the—"

A detonation in the office finished her sentence. Debris flew out the office door to smash against the concrete hallway and destroy of photo of Jacob and Wallace fishing.

Wallace hooked an arm around her and they retreated into the living room, just in time to avoid another explosion that sounded like a stun grenade. Jana figured they had thrown that through the office window and into the corridor in advance of their assault.

Even around the corner and ten feet away the sound left a hard ringing in her ears. Hiding behind the doorway, she strained to hear above the din, but couldn't make out any sounds.

She counted to five, pulled out a grenade, and tossed it into the hallway.

A shout, then the grenade went off. An instant later, Jana and Tyler burst back into the front hallway. One man lay motionless, a torn mess just inside the front door. Another was dragging himself through the rubble into the office, leaving a trail of blood behind him.

A man popped through the front door, leading with his gun. Jana shot him, and he pirouetted and fell. An instant later another attacker came through the office door and Tyler took him out.

The CIA field office director jerked his head, and they got back into the living room.

Tyler's instincts were correct. A moment later, another stun grenade went off in the front hall.

They want to capture us, Jana realized. *They want to capture us so Dr. Farag can torture us.*

Together they crept to rear of the living room, where Jana took a post at the doorway to the kitchen and Tyler overturned a heavy oak coffee table and got prone behind it. As he did so, Jana saw a steel plate bolted to the bottom.

Damn. Jacob thought of everything. I wish he was here.

She glanced at the security screen, but it had gone blank. They had either disabled it or one of the explosions took out the circuitry.

Jana gave a harder glance at the kitchen window. The sun was in that direction, and so she had lowered the Venetian blinds that morning. A group of terrorists had approached the house from that side.

She crouched, getting out of line of sight from the window behind a large counter in the middle of the kitchen. She hoped it was reinforced like the coffee table. Knowing Jacob, it probably was.

Her instincts proved correct. A couple of seconds later, the window blew in with a deafening roar. While the counter saved her, it couldn't protect her from the chunks of bulletproof glass, cutlery, and dishes that flew across the room. The dishes shattered into a thousand pieces, some of it rebounding off the wall and stinging Jana with a dozen little cuts. One large butcher knife ricocheted off the wall and planted itself into the counter inches from Jana's head.

Reeling from the shockwave, Jana managed to stagger to her feet and spray the shattered window just as two men rose into view.

They toppled backwards. Behind her, she heard a roar of gunfire in the living room. Jana kept herself hidden beside the open doorway and focused on the window.

A moment later, a terrible boom erupted in the kitchen. Jana was knocked back against the wall and then onto her knees. The ringing in her ears from before now doubled in intensity. Nevertheless, she stayed conscious and held onto her weapon.

A stun grenade. One of the guys I shot had a stun grenade. It must have blown up outside.

If it had blown up in here, it would be all over.

It was almost over anyway. The firing in the living room increased in intensity, and anyone outside the kitchen window would only have to lob a stun grenade inside without exposing themselves and she would be knocked flat.

She rushed the window before that could happen, her steps unsteady from the shock, stumbling over the heaps of debris.

Jana checked her pockets. She had already used her one fragmentation grenade, so she chucked a stun grenade out the window to buy herself some time.

Time was running out. The intruders were coming at the building from three different directions and while it sounded like Wallace was holding his own out there, the two of them were seriously ungunned. At least the windows in the living room faced a sheer cliff. Unless they had rock climbers among them, they wouldn't be hitting them from that direction.

And she and Wallace wouldn't be escaping from that direction either. They were trapped.

After the stun grenade went off, Jana aimed out the window and put a few rounds into the chest of a man lying half-conscious nearby. It felt cruel, but they were playing for keeps, and these guys were in a terrorist group trying to build a nuclear weapon.

Six months ago, she couldn't have brought herself to do that.

Six months ago seemed like a life lived by another person.

Bullets cracking off the windowsill made her duck back. Someone further away from the blast had nearly gotten her.

Another stun grenade went off, this time in the living room.

Head spinning, ears ringing, Jana stumbled over to the doorway and saw Tyler, his shirt soaked with blood from a gunshot to the shoulder, blearily reloading his weapon from behind the safety of the table, his hands fumbling through the simple movements. He hadn't been in the direct shockwave of that stun grenade, and neither had she, but the cumulative effect of them had almost overpowered them.

Jana aimed at the entrance from the front hall into the living room. Three dead bodies told her Tyler Wallace hadn't been slouching.

A terrorist showed himself. Jana fired at him, missed, and he bobbed back out of sight.

Something told her to turn around, and she was just in time to see someone at the window raising a gun. She fired at him and missed again. At least he ducked back down without firing an answering shot.

It was only a matter of moments now. They'd toss in another grenade, and that would be it. Or they'd take them out with bullets. She and Tyler had inflicted so many casualties on them that they might not be trying to capture them anymore. That would be better. She'd rather die than fall into their hands.

And she knew that that fate would not be long in coming.

***

Jacob's first inkling that something was wrong back home came when he saw a faint curl of smoke rising up over the rocky hill with its scattering of olive trees that blocked the view of his house.

He was driving along the winding seaside highway, the same one where he had raced the other direction to try and save Gabriella not so many months ago. He had just passed the restaurant where the bomb went off a couple of miles back. They had fixed it up within a matter of weeks so that no visible sign of the attack remained. All that was left was the bitter memory and a guilt he knew would never go away.

And now something strange was going on at or near his house.

He picked up speed. This road was little-used, which is why he had decided to live here, and only a truck lumbered past, going in the other direction.

He glanced at the driver, whose face remained placid. He obviously hadn't seen anything, but then again Jacob's house was out of sight from the main road, down a little lane marked private and hidden by a large outcropping of rock.

Jacob put on some speed and studied the blue sky above his house. He didn't see any smoke anymore. Had he imagined it?

If his house was under attack, wouldn't that trucker have heard gunfire? Maybe not over the sound of his own engine and the music he was probably playing.

Jacob gripped the wheel, poised for action. He had to assume something was going down. And that meant an attack. And if there was an attack, the attackers would post a sentry overlooking the road.

Taking out a sentry would cost time, and if Jana was in danger, he needed to get there now.

He'd have to take a chance.

Jacob hunkered low in his seat, cut his speed, and waited for the inevitable.

It came at the next turn. A bullet smacked through the window, leave a gaping hole and a spiderweb of cracks all around.

Even expecting it, he flinched, skidded onto the gravel by the side of the road, and had to yank hard on the wheel to get back on the asphalt.

A second bullet thunked against the engine block. A hiss and a jet of steam from the bullet hole told him he wouldn't make it very much further.

That was all right. He was almost there.

A third bullet took out his back window, spraying him with fragments of glass. He had passed the sentry, and the guy was firing at his rear now.

He screeched around the turn to his home and sped down the driveway.

As he did, he saw he was entering a battlefield.

The windows were all out, several bodies of men in balaclavas lay scattered around his lawn, and the sound of gunfire roared from inside his house.

Where had Jana gotten all that firepower? Had she discovered his cache of weapons?

The sight of Tyler Wallace's Mercedes with its tinted windows parked next to the house told him the answer. Tyler had helped design this house.

Great timing, sir.

Jacob screeched to a halt and leapt out, his 9mm at the ready. No one fired at him. It appeared the entire assault team was inside. It sure as hell sounded like it.

That sentry would be shifting position soon, and he was a good shot. Time to get inside.

He ran in a zigzag pattern toward his shattered front door, not even slowing down as he scooped up an UZI from one of the dead attackers. The gunfire inside intensified, followed by a thud of a flash-bang grenade.

They want to capture her, like last time.

He came to the front hall just as three men, all dressed in identical black and their backs to him, rushed through the doorway into the living room. He mowed them down with a long burst from the UZI.

Jacob got to the doorway and dared a peek. His living room was a wreck, the bulletproof coffee table overturned as a last stand. Jana was firing to his right, toward the kitchen. Tyler rose up and fired with a pistol, his other arm useless thanks to a shoulder wound.

He swung to the right, gazing past a carpet of bodies, and fired a burst the next time one of them showed themselves. The first guy to do so doubled over and fell, whether from his own bullets or those of his friends, he didn't know.

For a second, no one else came out of the kitchen. Jana and Tyler spotted him and grinned. Well, Tyler grinned. Jana looked relieved.

Still no one coming from that doorway. Jacob glanced over his shoulder to make sure no one was sneaking up on him. Nope. Jana and Tyler had taken care of them all.

Then, a grenade flew out of the kitchen doorway and landed right behind the coffee table where his lover and his boss were hiding.

CHAPTER NINE

Jacob's heart clenched, a cold feeling spreading in his gut as he knew there was no way for them to dodge and no way for him to get there in time.

Tyler Wallace popped up again, grenade in hand, and hurled it back into the kitchen before dropping down behind the table again. Jacob took cover too.

The grenade went off, and Jacob tore around the corner, UZI in one hand and 9mm pistol in the other.

He burst into the kitchen and found no one left to kill. Several bodies lay on the floor. Out the shattered window, he saw a couple of guys disappear over the brow of the nearest hill.

He looked back in the living room. "You guys OK?"

Jana and Tyler pointed to their ears and shrugged.

Jacob saw the blast pattern of a couple of flash-bang grenades and understood. These guys had wanted to incapacitate them and take them prisoner.

Once again, his job had endangered people he cared about.

Swallowing his guilt, he made the rounds of the house and found them all dead. A couple of the wounded he discovered in the final spasms of cyanide poisoning.

They had taken poison rather than be taken prisoner.

A standard practice of The Order.

They had found him at his secret residence, a place known only by a few.

There was only one answer to how they could have done that.

Aaron Peters' worst fears had come true.

The CIA had been compromised.

He returned to the house to find Jana patching up Tyler Wallace with a First Aid kit Jacob kept in the bedroom.

"We got to go," he shouted so they could hear him. "They might regroup and come back. And the cops are sure to. Jana, finish patching him up. I got to grab some things."

He rushed to his bedroom, opened a hidden wall safe, and removed cash and a few passports. Then he stocked up on guns and grenades from the arsenal and, burdened by equipment, hurried back to the living room.

"How the hell did they find this place?" Wallace asked.

"We'll talk in the car. Give me your keys. Mine took a bullet in the engine."

Wallace gave him his keys, and they hurried to the station director's Mercedes.

As they helped him into the back, possibilities raced through Jacob's mind.

Who could it have been? Who was the mole? He wasn't sure who knew about this place. Wallace did, and so did his personal assistant. Plus, a couple of CIA architects brought in from the States to fortify the building. Who else?

They must have been watching from that sentry point. It had a view of the road but not the house. When they saw the Mercedes pull up, they probably thought he was driving it. Those tinted windows kept them from seeing who was inside, and Wallace got into the house before they realized it wasn't him.

So they hadn't seen him leave in a Camaro, so when a vehicle came, they assumed it was Jacob and Jana. So Jacob's timely arrival came as a complete surprise.

Good. That gave them a bloody nose. It wouldn't stop them, though.

They'd be back.

"You got any place safe?" Jacob asked as he peeled out down the driveway, keeping low in case that sentry was still around.

"I thought this was," Wallace said through teeth gritted in pain.

"Well, it isn't."

"If it isn't, we can't trust any safe house," his boss said.

"True enough. Got any place the CIA doesn't know about?"

"I know someone who can put us up."

"Someone the CIA doesn't know about?"

"Sure."

"Good."

"Follow the coastal highway for twenty miles, then turn inland. I'll lead you."

Jacob studied him in the rearview mirror. They had passed the sentry point with no gunfire. The Order had retreated for the moment.

"You going to still be with me twenty miles from now?"

"This is nothing. Just drive. And while you're at it, tell me what you know and what you've been up to."

Jacob hesitated. The CIA had a leak. While he couldn't believe for one second that Tyler Wallace was that leak, he wasn't sure if he should tell Wallace about The Order or the fact that it had obviously infiltrated the CIA.

What if the car was bugged? What if Wallace told someone he thought he could trust who turned out to be the mole?

No, it was too risky. They had to go it alone, at least for the moment.

So as he drove and his boss clutched his shoulder in the back seat, Jacob spun a tale about how an operative from The Sword of the Righteous tracked Jana down at the national library and tried to murder her. They had fled, using fake passports Jacob bought on the black market, but obviously the guy he bought them from was in the know or the terrorists, anticipating the move, tracked him down and made him talk. Then an operative must have tailed them to the house and gone back to report the location and bring in a full hit team.

All the while, Jana kept giving him sidelong looks. She didn't say a word.

Once Jacob was done, the car settled into silence.

"Worked fast," Wallace said at last, holding his shoulder and looking out the back window to check on any tails. "You've been in Greece less than two days."

"The group has cells in Turkey, and you know how porous the border is in this country."

"Strange that they tried to kill Jana in France, and then tried to capture the two of you here. They must have thought my car was yours. But why the change in objective?"

"Dunno."

More silence.

"Turn left up here," Wallace said. "You'll come to a dirt road on your right. Take it all the way up to the top of the hill."

"Who is this we're going to see?" Jacob asked, glad for the change of topic.

"A friend."

Well, I guess you can have secrets too.

The road wended its way up the hill to a round stone tower with whitewashed walls that shone in the sun. Jacob realized it had once been a windmill, now converted into a private home. A battered old van was parked outside. An olive grove stood on a plateau beyond. As they parked and got out, they heard wind chimes.

A woman in a white dress opened the door and stepped out. She was Greek, in her late forties or early fifties, and still retained a natural beauty. She waved and gave a warm smile, running toward the car.

She stopped abruptly when Jacob got out.

"Who are you?" she asked in Greek. "Where's Tyler?"

Tyler eased himself out of the back seat.

"Here, honey."

Honey?

The woman's eyes went wide. "Again?"

Again?

She rushed over, gave Wallace a hug around his uninjured shoulder, followed by a kiss. Jacob stood by, suddenly awkward. He knew Wallace had an ex-wife and a couple of kids back in the States. He knew nothing about his private life here. In the CIA, people tended not to ask personal questions. If someone didn't offer the information, you assumed it wasn't your business.

"Come inside," she said, leading him along. She glanced at Jacob. "You must be Jacob."

She didn't say that like it was a good thing.

"Um, yes."

The woman nodded toward Jana, who had just stepped out of the car. "Is she another … never mind. Don't tell me. Come on inside."

She led Wallace into the old windmill. Now that the adrenaline from the fight had worn off and he had gotten to safety, Wallace had deflated. He was dragging his feet, shoulders hunched.

"We need to get a doctor," Jacob said.

"I am a doctor," the Greek woman said.

They entered the ground floor, a large circular room made up of a kitchen and dining room separated by a counter. It was furnished with rustic old wooden furniture. A spiral staircase wound up the interior wall to disappear into the next floor above.

Jacob looked at his boss, worried. "I'm glad you are, ma'am, but the bullet is still inside him. He needs to—"

"And he'll get that. Now clear the dining room table." She turned to Jana and switched to English. "You. Wash your hands thoroughly and then go to the bottom drawer of that cupboard over there. Grab an oil cloth and a white sheet and spread them over the table."

“You’re going to operate here?” Jacob said, clearing off the remains of the woman’s lunch.

“No, I’m going to make love to him while the two of you watch. What do you think?”

Jacob kept quiet.

After they had cleared the table and covered it, the woman ran upstairs and returned with a medical bag.

“Get him on the table and strip him to the waist while I get ready,” she ordered.

She still hadn’t introduced herself. Jacob figured her name wasn’t going to be part of her hospitality. And she kept giving Jacob nasty looks.

What, is it my fault we got attacked?

Well, kind of, I guess.

As they settled Wallace on the table and cut away his shirt with a pair of scissors their angry hostess gave them, the station director spoke.

“I was coming to chew you out for going dark, but now I see it’s the only way for you guys to be safe. You need to get out of Greece. You on the trail of the Egyptian doctor?”

“Yes. We were going to leave the country the day after tomorrow, but we’ll go tonight. Not everything’s prepped yet, so we’ll lay low until it is.”

Vasiliki Castellanos had told him he’d get his colleague to get him the credentials so that he and Jana could make it to the auction. That would take time, however, and they didn’t have time. As long as they were in Greece, they were unsafe.

“Take my car,” Wallace said. “You can be over the border by sundown. Don’t tell me where you’re going. It’s obvious we have a mole. Looks like going dark was your best option. Also gets me off the hook with the higher-ups who were breathing down my neck wanting to know where you were.” Wallace let out a chuckle. “Now give me my phone. I need to make some calls. We got to get the ambassador to stop the police from searching the house, although they’re probably there by now, and we need a clean-up crew to clear it of any sensitive evidence.”

As Wallace made his calls, his girlfriend set out her surgical instruments and made Jacob and Jana wash their hands.

“You’re assisting,” she told them.

Jacob wasn't about to disagree. This woman was scary, and she looked seriously pissed.

They got to work giving Tyler Wallace tabletop surgery. The old Marine insisted on only local anesthetic.

"Got to keep my mind as clear as I can," he said. "Something big is going down and we got some serious problems in the CIA."

You can say that again, old buddy.

CHAPTER TEN

Dr. Moswen Farag studied the small island the motor launch was taking them to. With him were five of the best fighters of The Sword of the Righteous, watched over closely by three heavily armed bodyguards.

George Dawson's bodyguards.

The bodyguards—burly Catalans who carried themselves like ex-military—had met them in Gibraltar and told them that the auction was actually happening on Dawson's private island off the Spanish coast.

Farag wasn't surprised by this, and was even less surprised at the strip search the bodyguards gave them. He had anticipated this, and the five men he had picked to accompany him were all experts in unarmed combat. Of them, his righthand man Hamza was the best.

They were brought to a motor launch in Gibraltar's port, Farag looking longingly at the British warships moored nearby. How he would love to sink them. His gaze swept up from the sunny port to the British city stuck on a little peninsula jutting out of the Spanish coast, the terrain rising to a giant rocky outcropping atop which stood an old fort and many modern missile installations.

This was how the British controlled the Strait of Gibraltar, the doorway between the Atlantic and the Mediterranean. Morocco, visible as a brown line dotted with white houses to the south, controlled it as well, but they were outgunned by the British, who could call on all of Europe to back them up if Muslims tried to control this vital waterway that was rightfully theirs.

Typical. The unbelievers had always curtailed the power of the Muslim world.

Not for long, though. No, not for long.

Now they sped along the Spanish coastline, passing coast guard vessels, fishing trawlers, and numerous pleasure craft. They blended in with no problem, and they all carried fake Spanish passports acquired for them by brothers in that country. They had nothing to worry about from the authorities.

What worried Dr. Farag were the other bidders. He had no idea who they might be.

Soon, the boat turned toward a tiny island. It didn't look more than a few acres in size, little more than a rock. Dawson had cultivated it, though, adding an olive grove and a walled garden as well as a large glass and steel mansion in the modern style.

The millionaire collector's private playground. Farag wondered what sinful things happened here, away from prying eyes.

The boat entered a little cove and docked next to a yacht. It looked a lot smaller than Dawson's wealth could afford, but nothing bigger could fit in this confined space.

At the end of the pier, flanked by a pair of bodyguards, stood Dawson. He was a tall, full-bodied man in a white suit and matching wide-brimmed hat. The face under that hat was flabby, with a red nose and weak blue eyes. A typical dissipated Westerner. Probably drank whiskey and slept with whores every night. Well, Allah would soon judge him. Dr. Farag would see to that.

"Greetings!" Dawson said in English. "Welcome to my little sanctuary."

"Pleased to meet you, Mr. Dawson," Dr. Farag replied as he alighted. He did not offer his hand—he didn't want to touch this filthy sinner—and Dawson didn't offer it.

"I am sure you are pressed for time so why don't you come up to my viewing room. One of the other bidders is already here, and we will soon fetch the third bidder. They haven't made it to Gibraltar port yet, but we expect them shortly."

Dawson led them up a path toward the mansion, passing through an open ironwork gate into a lovely five-acre garden inside the walls. Dr. Farag couldn't help but look around in admiration. Dawson had turned a patch of this rock into a paradise.

The former Egyptologist soon turned his attention back to the business at hand. Dawson was leading them to a small windowless outbuilding, more of an oversized shed, next to the main house.

"I keep most of my collection in the house. Perhaps you would like to see it once you've looked at the Staff of Ra?"

"Certainly."

They entered the outbuilding, and Dr. Farag stopped short.

Because not only did he see a couple of bodyguards toting submachineguns, which he had expected, and the Staff of Ra lying in a display case, which until this moment he was uncertain he'd actually find here, but he also saw four members of the Jihad of the Sahel, an Islamist group based in Libya.

Well, they called themselves Islamist, but most of the leadership used to be officials in the old government of that godless hypocrite, Muammar Gaddafi.

The Jihad of the Sahel were nothing but bandits posing as Allah's warriors.

Their leader, a son of a dog named Marwan Issa, a little jackal of a desert warrior who used to run one of Gaddafi's prison hellholes, treated them to a smile.

"Dr. Farag, the famous Egyptologist! So pleased to meet you. Are you here to worship the pagan gods of your country?"

"No, I'm here to outbid you and take what's rightfully mine."

Issa laughed. "We have deep pockets too, Farag. We have some new sponsors, wise men of God who don't like your sledgehammer tactics."

Dawson raised his hands. "Gentleman, let's leave the competitiveness to the bidding, shall we?"

"This fool made life hard for all of us," Issa growled. "We lost two of our bases to airstrikes."

"At least the infidels are good for something," Dr. Farag said with a smile.

"You are nothing but a pagan fool!" Issa shouted.

One of the guards cleared his throat. Issa and Farag both looked in his direction. His submachinegun, which he had held sloped, had moved a fraction of an inch closer to the ready position.

Dawson, smiling, stepped between them.

"It must be quite a thrill for both of you to see the object of your quest after so long."

How long have these false holy warriors been searching for the Staff of Ra? Dr. Farag wondered.

He had no idea they had even known what it was.

But he couldn't dwell on that for long. Dawson's words had a riveting effect on him, and his gaze turned to the object on the table. It lay inside a clear box of radiation shielding glass.

The staff was almost identical to the one he had uncovered in the Sudan. A bit smaller, perhaps, but in far better condition. The lead sheath was unbroken as far as he could see, and the collimator, while distorted and made useless by the weight of sand on top of it for so many centuries, seemed complete.

Dr. Farag cast a nervous look over the protective casing. Radiation was a silent killer, one that snuck into your DNA and wreaked havoc on it, leading to horrible cancers or deformities in your children. He had already taken a dose of radiation in the Sudan, and the last thing he wanted to do was get another.

Stay strong in your faith, you weakling. Allah will protect you. You are doing great work for Him.

"You mentioned a third team of bidders?" Dr. Farag asked, scratching his ear. One of this men rounded the case to take a look at the Staff of Ra from another angle.

"They are expected at the docks shortly," their host replied. "When they arrive, we will send the motor launch to pick them up."

"So these … " Dr. Farag gestured at the Libyans " … these are the only other bidders?"

"Yes. A select community."

He scratched his ear again. Another of his men pulled out a cigarette and asked a guard for a light. Hamza shifted to look at the case from the other side.

"When will the motor launch leave?"

"As soon as we get a call from them. I understand your impatience. I'm sure they won't be long."

"NOW!" Dr. Farag shouted.

He dropped to the floor.

His five followers sprang into action. The man who had rounded the display case had done so to get closer to the guard at the far end of the room. He spun, landing a kick square into the man's jaw, which gave way with a terrible snap. Another of his followers flipped another guard. The third guard blocked an attack from one of his men and fired a burst into his gut, only to get taken out by a punch to the throat by Hamza.

Issa and his followers from The Jihad of the Sahel ran for the door. No one stopped them. Dr. Farag's men were too busy with the guards.

Within seconds, all of Dawson's men were down, the collector cringing in a corner. Dr. Farag had lost only one man. The survivors loaded up on the guard's guns and stormed out of the display area. Dr. Farag grabbed a pistol and covered Dawson. Within moments, they were alone.

He smiled at the collector as he heard gunshots ring out across the property. His men would clear the rest of the island, and the Staff of Ra would be his.

"D-don't hurt me!" Dawson wailed, shivering like a mass of jelly.

“I won’t. I promise.” *At least not until we have secured the island. Then I’ll shoot you like the dog you are.*

“Who is the third party who are coming?”

“A Canadian couple. They are members of an Aryan group there.”

Dr. Farag snorted. White supremacists. What idiots. Humanity’s great struggle wasn’t about race. It was about religion. If a man engaged in jihad, the color of his skin didn’t matter. The true faith was the only thing that mattered.

After a couple of minutes, his men returned. Only two of them. That was enough.

“The guards put up some tough resistance,” Hamza reported. “Mohammed and Ibrahim were martyred. Issa and his cowards took the motor launch and got away.”

Dr. Farag cursed. “It would have been good to kill them, but it doesn’t matter. We have what we came for.”

He shot Dawson in the head without a moment’s thought.

“Let’s put on our Tyvek suits and get this loaded on Dawson’s yacht. Now we have all we need.”

As Dr. Farag and his men prepared to remove the Libyan Staff of Ra from its protective case, his mind grew troubled. While Issa was a mercenary and a false jihadist, he was no coward. Why had he run so quickly? It wasn’t like him. Being a desert tribesman from the Fezzan, fighting was in his blood. He should have taken advantage of the chaos to grab a gun from one of the guards or one of Dr. Farag’s men, and yet he ran.

No matter. They had what they came for. Within a few days, they'd place the fissile material into the bomb they had prepared, and then they could pick a target.

London? Berlin? The possibilities were as endless as they were enticing. Smuggling routes and the availability of transportation would determine their choice, but in the end the target didn’t really matter.

A nuclear explosion in a European capital would start a war between Christianity and Islam that would set the world on fire.

CHAPTER ELEVEN

As they approached Dawson's island in a rented motorboat, Jana studied it with increasing concern. They had been late getting to Gibraltar thanks to a truck that had flipped on the highway and blocked the road. It had been ridiculous. A vital secret mission delayed by traffic! On the phone, Dawson had assured them that he would hold off the auction until they got there. Posing as rich Canadian white supremacists, and with the help of Jacob's contact vouching for them, they had convinced the millionaire that they were viable contenders for purchasing the Staff of Ra.

So why wasn't Dawson there waiting to meet them at the port? And why wasn't he answering his calls anymore?

"There aren't any boats in the dock," Jacob said from the helm as he peered toward the little cove they aimed for. "Something's gone wrong."

"You sure we're at the right place?"

"Are you going to turn into a backseat driver?"

"Har har. Where could they be?"

Jacob shrugged.

Jana checked their guns as Jacob pulled into the cove and docked at the pier. No one was in sight. As he cut the engine, all Jana could hear was the sea breeze and the cry of gulls.

"I got a bad feeling about this," Jana said.

"Me too. Be careful."

"If I was careful, I wouldn't be in a relationship with you."

"I hope those aren't the last words I hear on this Earth."

They came across the first body on the path from the marina to the house. A large Spanish man lay on his back, three gunshot wounds to the chest. He had no weapon but he had all the hallmark of a bodyguard. Several shell casings around him showed he had been firing at someone.

Jacob and Jana had been warned they would be frisked and disarmed before taking the motor launch. So, had one of the bodyguards turned on the others? Or had one of the other bidders snuck weapons onto the island somehow?

They kept going, feeling exposed on the rocky terrain that offered little cover, up toward a house within a walled garden. The gate stood open, another dead Spaniard lying in front of it.

They crept into an enclosed garden and saw a lovely home surrounded by greenery. An outbuilding next to it had its door hanging open. Several bodies were visible inside.

They entered and found a radiation-proof container standing in the center of the room, open and empty.

Jacob surveyed the bodies all around it. He pointed to an older gentleman with a hideous head wound.

"That's Dawson. I recognize him from his file photo." He pointed to an Arab man lying nearby. "I recognize this guy from the files too. He's a known operative for The Sword of the Righteous."

They headed to the main house and found no one inside, just a well-appointed holiday home with one major exception—a large exhibition room filled with Nazi and Holocaust memorabilia. Jana recognized several items from Dawson's website.

Jana clicked her tongue. While all history was interesting and needed to be preserved, this display wasn't history. It felt like some sick form of pornography. She didn't feel bad that Dawson was dead. The world was better off without him.

What did bother her was that The Sword of the Righteous now had the Staff of Ra. They had found three dead Arabs, but Dr. Farag wasn't among them.

"We need to get out of here," she told Jacob. "This is a race against time and we're lagging way behind. We have no idea where they could have gone."

"When we spoke to Dawson on the phone, he said the others were already there. Others. Plural. So it isn't just The Sword of the Righteous that came here."

"Who else could it have been?"

Jacob rubbed his chin and looked around at all the Nazi memorabilia. "I don't know, but I have an idea. And luckily we don't have to go very far to find them."

***

Sitting in his safehouse, an isolated farm a few miles north of the Spanish port of Algeciras, right across the bay from Gibraltar, Dr. Farag stared at the Staff of Ra and wondered.

The more he thought about it, the more the headlong flight of Marwan Issa and his men seemed strange. It had been bothering him on the boat ride out of Dawson's private island, then along the coast to their rendezvous with the local cell of holy warriors, who had picked them and the Staff of Ra up in another boat. They scuttled Dawson's boat, got to shore, and took the truck waiting for them to this old stone farmhouse amid the sunny cultivated fields of southern Spain.

"Why would they run?" he asked Hamza. "It makes no sense."

"They're cowards," the bigger man grunted.

Dr. Farag resisted the urge to roll his eyes. Hamza was not what you would call a towering genius. A great warrior of Allah, but not exactly a deep thinker.

"No, Hamza. They are corrupt, they are unbelievers, but they are not cowards. Issa is a veteran of many battles, and I'm sure his followers are too. And they must have gone through as much research and preparation as we did to know the value of the Staff of Ra. So why flee without a fight? They didn't even try to grab a gun. They did nothing but run!"

"Cowards," Hamza grunted again.

Dr. Farag suppressed a sigh. "No, my friend. They ran for some other reason. But what? The Staff of Ra was right before them."

Or was it?

Dr. Farag grabbed a Geiger counter off the shelf.

"Suit up," he told Hamza. "We need to check something."

They got on their Tyvek suits and went to the barn, where one of the greatest archaeological discoveries of the century was hidden beneath a pile of hay.

Moving awkwardly because of the heavy suits, they opened up the radiation-proof carrying case that Dawson had made for the staff. Even though he was safe in his suit, Dr. Farag felt a little shudder pass through his body. He passed the Geiger counter over the staff.

"Nothing," he said. "No radiation."

"You said there would be any radiation if the lead casing was complete."

Dr. Farag nodded. "That is true. I'm surprised there isn't at least a little leak after all these years."

He hesitated, not sure what to do next. He hated to test further, but he had to make sure. So much relied on this.

Summoning his courage, he said, “Take your knife and pry open the edge of the lead casing between the collimator and the shaft.”

Hamza looked at him, surprised. “Are you sure?”

“Yes. We have to be certain.”

Hamza shrugged and did as he was told, digging with the tip through the soft lead until he made a little hole. He began to expand it, the dull gray uranium showing through.

“That’s enough,” Dr. Farag said.

He tried the Geiger counter again.

Nothing. Not a trace of radiation.

Dr. Farag roared and threw the Geiger counter against the wall.

“It’s a fake! He tricked us! That unbeliever tricked us!”

Hamza gaped at him, then looked at the staff.

“But it looks just like the other one. A perfect replica. How did he know what the original looked like?”

"Who's to say? Maybe he came across an old papyrus that described it or an old carving that depicted it. He was well-connected in collector's circles. He might have come across something like that."

Hamza smiled. “I am glad you killed him.”

“So am I, but that doesn’t help our situation.”

“So what do we do?”

Dr. Farag thought for a minute. Hamza stood staring at him. He found that blank look through the protective mask distracting and resisted the urge to shout at him. Hamza might be loyal, but he wasn’t the kind of person you could shout at.

The solution, or part of a solution, popped into his head. He snapped his fingers, or at least tried to. His heavy rubber gloves simply made a brushing sound.

“I know! Before I found clues to locate the site of the temple in Ibn Balamon, I was following a different line of inquiry. It is said the great Nazi general Erwin Rommel excavated many ancient sites in North Africa. The Nazis were especially interested in Egyptian sites. That’s why we found evidence of the statue in Libya having been uncovered some time before. It was excavated by Rommel’s men. They got the Libyan Staff of Ra.”

“But the war, they were defeated. Why didn’t the Allies get the staff? Do you think maybe the Russians got it?”

“No. Rumor has it that it was hidden in Italy. I was close to the answer of where it might have been hidden when I came across a simpler way to get a staff—the location of the Sudanese temple. But I can go back to my original research.”

“That will take time, and every day we spend in Europe we risk getting caught. They are looking for us.”

“I know that, but it might not take as much time as you think. Before I discovered the link to Ibn Balamon, I had a theory where the secret cave might be. I didn’t follow it up, though, because a raid into the Sudan proved to be easier.”

“Italians are soft. What’s so difficult about finding this cave?”

Dr. Farag shook his head. “It’s not so much the country the cave is in, it’s what it is beneath that makes searching for it difficult.”

CHAPTER TWELVE

Jacob really, really didn't want to make this call.

A few years before, he had been assigned to help break up a neo-Nazi group in southern Italy called the Sons of Mussolini that was building a bomb. They planned to blow up a migrant camp and plant evidence that the Jewish community did it so that the mostly Muslim migrants would attack the Jews. Jacob had been called in because there had been a crisis in another sector that pulled a bunch of operatives away from Europe, and the CIA team in Italy was shorthanded.

The Sons of Mussolini, as their name implied, harkened back to the days of Italian fascism, which actually came into power and lasted longer than German fascism. Italian fascism was full of symbolism of the past. Mussolini fancied himself a new Roman emperor who would revive the old empire. Its members were fascinated with all things ancient, creating a Eurocentric foundation myth in which white people were at the top of a racial food chain with the Italians at the very peak.

This ideology was mostly espoused by the elite officers in the organization. The rank and file, recruited from the riffraff of Italian prisons and football hooligan clubs, just liked getting drunk and beating up immigrants, Jews, and gay people.

It was a quick operation. With the aid of the Italian police, they surrounded the house where the group was working on the bomb, lobbed in some tear gas, and stormed the building. Two skinheads were killed, and the rest surrendered.

The only problem was, the raid only bagged some foot soldiers and the two chemists building the bomb. The more senior members of the Sons of Mussolini had been tipped off. The Italian police tracked down a couple of them in the following weeks, but many key individuals went underground and eluded capture. Jacob had heard through the grapevine that they were reforming.

He had also heard they had a rich source of funding. The Sons of Mussolini was now the richest neo-Nazi organization in Europe. He could think of no one else with enough cash to have piqued Dawson's interest in the auction.

The problem was, he had no idea where the Sons of Mussolini were based these days. He had only been brought in as a replacement for another operative, hadn't been in on the initial investigation, and hadn't kept up with it since.

And the only way he could find out was to call Tyler Wallace.

Wallace had encouraged him to go dark. Both men saw that as the safest thing, and here he was having to make a call to a CIA phone. All CIA phones were monitored by the organization. If there really was a mole, he or she might find out.

No choice. Gritting his teeth, he made the call.

"What the hell are you calling me for?" Tyler demanded. He didn't even say hello.

"How are you?"

"Recovering and getting a foot massage in a converted windmill. Why are you calling?"

Jacob smiled.

"The cleanup crew dealing with my house?"

"Don't worry about that. How are things with you?"

"Could be better, so basically the same as always. I need to know the current HQ of the Sons of Mussolini."

"Um, all right. I'll look that up and get back to you."

Jacob heard the tapping of a keyboard. Wallace might be getting a foot massage from his lovely doctor friend, but he still had work close to hand.

"Taranto," Wallace said. "It's a house on 24 Via Galeso."

Jacob nodded. Taranto was in the very south of Italy, at the top of the bootheel. It would have been an important port for the Italian Navy during the North African campaign.

"Thanks a lot," Jacob told his boss. "Feel better."

"Mmm-hmm. At least my feet feel good. You take care."

Jacob laughed and hung up.

He turned to Jana. "Looks like we're going back to Italy."

"Too bad we keep using different passports. I could make a killing on frequent flier miles."

***

Via Galeso paralleled the shoreline of Taranto's inner harbor, not far from the 15th century castle that guarded its entrance. Most of the homes and apartment buildings were much newer that, mostly ugly concrete blocks put up right after the war, with more modern glass and steel buildings interspersed between them. Taranto had been heavily bombed during the war, leveling entire blocks of old buildings.

Jacob's eyes darted all around as he and Jana strolled down the residential street, trying to look like tourists. All he saw were real tourists and Italians going about their business.

They came to number 24, a large house and a rare survival of the nineteenth century, the kind that are often subdivided into apartments. From their vantage point across the street, they could see the windows were shuttered and the threshold was dusty. A “for sale” sign hung from the low wall separating the small front yard from the street.

“Looks like your intel was wrong,” Jana whispered.

“Maybe. Pretend you’re interested in the house. Take a picture of the sign and then some of the house."

He crossed the street, Jana following. As she went through the motions of acting like a prospective buyer, Jacob opened the waist-high iron gate with a squeal of rusty hinges and walked casually up to the front door. He had learned that if you act like you belong, most civilians never looked twice.

A group of Italian neo-Nazis seeing someone stroll up to their hideout would be a different story. He kept an eye on the windows, expecting them to fly open at any moment.

They didn’t. He got to the door, palmed a lockpick from his pocket, and got the door open with a few seconds of fiddling.

Still acting casual, he opened the door and went inside.

Nothing but empty rooms and dusty floors. Jacob cursed.

He made a quick check of the upstairs just to make sure, then rejoined Jana outside.

"They've gone, and it looks like they've been gone for a while. The CIA's intel is old. With everything happening in the Middle East, they haven't been keeping tabs on the less lethal groups."

“They might get more lethal.”

“Yeah. I’m going to check on a member of the group. He’s not hardcore, but he has associated with them in the past and he’s sold us information to stay out of jail. He lives right here in Taranto.”

“How do you know he hasn’t moved too?”

“He can’t. He’s tied down to a business and I already checked that he’s still running it.”

***

Aaron Peters studied the documents for the twentieth time and considered his options.

He was still in Tunisia, liaising with a Tunisian anti-terrorism squad. The locals had located the safehouse of the cell that had planted the nightclub bomb. They launched a surprise raid and for once caught The Order unprepared. The two operatives in the house immediately trashed the laptops they were working on, flushed their phones down the toilet, and bit down on cyanide capsules, but in their haste they had missed another phone in one of the bedrooms, probably left by the man Aaron had killed on the beach.

Back at the Tunisian anti-terrorism squad's HQ, Aaron ran some decryption software and soon hacked into it. He found no one in the contacts list. The man had obviously memorized any numbers he needed.

Aaron did find some texts, though. Most were incomprehensible, a mishmash of acronyms, abbreviations that could stand for more than one word, and oblique references.

One stood out, though.

"Taranto. Cleaning team. J&J."

His blood curdled as he read it.

J&J. Jacob and Jana?

It dated from yesterday. The "cleaning team" (which could mean only one thing) was probably already there.

Taranto? Assuming the operative hadn't misspelled Toronto, the Canadian city, he meant Taranto, Italy.

Taranto … Taranto … why would they go there?

He had never been there, and he didn't recall any CIA operations there, but then again he had been off in the mountains of Afghanistan and Pakistan for several years and had little touch with operations in other sectors.

The important thing was that Jacob and Jana were headed there, and The Order knew about it.

He needed to get there as soon as he could, be he had the feeling that he wouldn't make it in time.

He'd have to call in the cavalry. Aaron put in a call to the CIA station director in Rome.

The local operatives backed by the Italian authorities could take care of it. Hopefully. He'd get on the first plane, though.

No way was he going to sit here in Tunisia while his daughter and mentee got targeted by The Order.

CHAPTER THIRTEEN

Jana loved bookstores, but she had a feeling she was going to hate this one.

From the exterior, it looked like any ordinary bookshop. Under a sign that read, “Taranto Books: New, Used, and Rare” was a window that displayed mostly old volumes on military history.

That was her first clue that this wasn’t her kind of place. Her next clues came when she entered and saw the two aisles in the long, narrow bookshop.

The military history books were almost entirely devoted to Mussolini’s invasion of Abyssinia and the campaigns in World War Two. A large political section held fascist tracts, and there was a section on Roman “history” that was mostly neo-fascist mythmaking. She recognized many of the names of hack historians who wanted to glorify the Roman Empire as some sort of whites-only ethnostate, when in fact the opposite had been true. Everyone from Syrians to Scots could be citizens of the Roman Empire.

But in the echo chamber that these “historians” had created, it was easy to think differently.

The man behind the counter was a slim little fellow in his late forties, his curly black hair touched with gray. His eyes widened when he saw Jacob come through the door.

“Hi, Garibaldi,” Jacob said in English. “Nice to see you again. Not.”

The bookseller looked nervously from Jacob to Jana and back again. “W-what do you want?”

Jacob shut the front door, locked it, and turned the sign from open to closed.

“I want to beat the living crap out of you. But you’re going to disappoint me and tell me everything I want to know. Please don’t tell me anything, because it would ruin my day not to stomp on your face.”

Garibaldi raised his hands, standing up. “I-I don’t want trouble.”

Jana noticed that his belt buckle had a portrait of Mussolini in relief.

“Let’s go to the back room,” Jacob said. “I don’t want anyone looking through your window and seeing me slap you silly.”

The bookseller followed, meek as a lamb. He was hardly the Aryan warrior depicted in so much far-right propaganda, and he certainly didn’t live up to his namesake, the hero of Italian independence.

Jana took up the rear, keeping a close eye on him, suspicious that it was all an act.

The back room was a combination office and storage room. Several boxes of books lay about. A chair, desk, and laptop were tucked in a corner. Beside it stood a bookshelf of old volumes and manuscripts.

“What are these?” Jana asked, indicating them.

“My personal collection.”

Jacob grabbed the chair, turned it around, and pushed Garibaldi into it. Jana noticed he had positioned the Italian with his back to the bookshelf. Jacob was skilled at picking up on subtle cues.

As Jacob grilled Garibaldi, she perused the shelves.

“Where did the Sons of Mussolini move their headquarters?”

“I don’t know.”

“Don’t give me that. You were a member.”

The volumes all seemed to date to just before or during the Second World War. Most were fascist tracts produced by the Mussolini regime. She pulled out one pamphlet and found it was a membership orientation booklet for new fascist party recruits.

“I was only an outer party member,” Garibaldi protested. “After the bomb raid, I quit.”

“Yeah, sure you did. Where did they move to?”

“I swear I don’t know.”

Jacob grabbed him by the throat. “I don’t have time for this!”

“Look. You know I was never in the inner circle. And I helped you before. Doesn’t that count for something?” Garibaldi’s voice shook so much he could barely get the words out.

“It’s keeping me from skipping rope with your entrails. Now tell me where they went.”

Jana crouched as she noticed the bottom shelf was mostly unpublished manuscripts and journals.

"I keep telling you, I don't know where the HQ is. After the raid, they went silent. The inner party members cut off contact with all the outer party members. Party members still come in sometimes, though. They like my store."

I bet they do, Jana thought.

“Do you know where any of them live?” Jacob asked.

Rummaging through these, she found many were government reports or military documents, probably worth a fortune on the collector’s market.

“They don’t say, and they only pay in cash. You can check my records if you want. What’s going on? Did they do something?”

“Why do you ask that?”

"I, um, well, you wouldn't be here if they hadn't done something."

“What do you know?”

“Nothing, really. Just some rumors. Hints they dropped when they’d buy books and we’d talk over a glass of wine.”

The manuscripts were double shelved. Jana began to search through the papers tucked in the back.

“Hints? What hints?” Jacob demanded.

“Just crazy stuff. Boasts. You wouldn’t be interested.”

“Try me.”

Garibaldi licked his lips and tried to look over his shoulder at Jana. Jacob slapped him. “Pay attention. What did they talk about?”

A small black, leather-bound volume caught her eye. She pulled it out and saw an eagle and swastika embossed on gold on the front. The symbol of the German Nazi party. Before she could open it, Garibaldi’s answer stopped her short.

“It’s a legend about an ancient Egyptian device called the Staff of Ra. It’s supposed to wield deadly power, frying its victims with the power of the Sun.”

Jesus! Does everyone know about this thing?

“And they want to get a hold of it?”

"Sure. They say it's in Italy. Rommel found it and shipped it over here during the retreat. They hid it somewhere, and it disappeared sometime during the war. It's never been found. They said some guy was trying to sell it on the black market, but it was a fake because the seller said he'd gotten it from North Africa, but he couldn't have, because Rommel took it from there eighty years ago."

Jana opened the journal and was surprised to see it written in Arabic.

The first line read, “I, Lieutenant Matteo Giordano, am writing this journal in Arabic so that none of my comrades can read it. I’d like to establish a record of the campaign to conquer North Africa for Il Duce and the greater glory of the Italian people. Long live Italy! Long live

Mussolini! I also want to make a record of the treasures and discoveries brought out from that region."

She closed the journal and tucked it in her pocket, skin prickling as she realized her luck. Scanning the bookshelf, she didn't see any other books in Arabic. Did Garibaldi even know how to read the language? A unlikely course of study for a white supremacist. He probably kept it simply for the Nazi symbol embossed on the cover.

Jacob questioned him for several more minutes, getting more vague references to the Staff of Ra and other supposed occult items the Nazis had collected, even the Spear of Longinus and the blueprint of a UFO that supposedly crashed during the siege of Stalingrad. It was all getting ridiculous, and Jacob soon lost interest when he realized this idiot had no idea where the Sons of Mussolini leadership had gotten to.

At last, her partner gave up, and with a final threat to come back, they left.

"What was that look of triumph I saw on your face a few minutes ago?" Jacob asked as they stepped onto the street.

"I'm not sure yet. Let's get back to the hotel room and I'll see."

***

Ten hours later, Jana shut the journal and sat back in the bed, where she had been lying propped up on pillows in the early predawn, absorbed in the old narrative of Nazi plunder taken from North Africa.

Lieutenant Matteo Giordano had been an officer in the Italian colonies of Tripolitania and Cyrenaica, what are now western and eastern Libya. Italy had taken the region from the Ottoman Empire in 1911 and performed extensive archeological excavations there. As an officer in the colonial administration, Giordano's job had been as a liaison between the military and local leaders, as well as recruiting Libyan men into the colonial army. He had been promoted several times due to his skills in the Arabic language.

When World War Two started, he had been attached to the North African Campaign as a translator and guide. His duties included going into villages and towns during Rommel's eastern push toward Egypt and looting any wealth from the local Jewish population—something for which he showed no remorse—as well as exploring archaeological sites. As the German and Italian army pushed closer to the Egyptian frontier, the high command grew more and more interested in what lay under the sand.

Eventually, the fascist army came to the oasis of Al Jaghbub in eastern Libya. This oasis had tactical importance because it was the first in a string of oases leading into Egypt, making for a viable invasion route through the Sahara. It also held an interest for the Gestapo, since the archaeologists they had brought along discovered a sizeable Egyptian ruin on a nearby hill.

Lieutenant Giordano was not an archaeologist, so he wasn't privy to the excavation, but he did note "a great excitement among the Gestapo and their team of archaeologists, and a deep secrecy about the site. Even though it made a good lookout and location for a radio transmitter, no one but they were allowed up there."

In an entry dated a couple of days after that one, the Italian lieutenant wrote, "More excitement among the archaeology crew. They returned to the oasis bearing a long box which they had constructed by nailing two ammunition crates end to end. Whatever they had in there was heavy and required four men to carry. It was immediately brought to the Gestapo house (they and the high command have taken the only decent homes in the oasis!) and posted a heavy guard. I suspect I will never see or hear about that box and its contents again."

That suspicion proved incorrect, as was shown in an entry dated more than a year later. It had taken hours of reading through Lieutenant Giordano's military adventures to come to another pertinent point in his narrative, but Jana Peters was used to trawling through oceans of data to find the jewel in the deep.

And what a jewel that turned out to be!

"We have made it to Taranto, and I do not think I will ever see the shores of North Africa again until this war is over. Our undermanned and undersupplied army is on the brink of defeat, and rumors I hear from men returning from the Eastern Front say that things are going bad in the struggle against the Soviets too. I'm glad to be writing this in Arabic, because if anyone in my unit could read this I would be sent to the camps for such defeatism. And yet, I have been a soldier for twenty years. How can I not see the impending disaster before my eyes?

"With us come the Gestapo and the archaeologists, who have a sealed van they had brought onto the ship. I wonder if that strange crate they were so excited about is inside? They have brought with them a team of Libyan laborers who do not look like they want to leave their homeland."

In an entry dated three days later, Jana hit the jackpot.

"The Gestapo have brought me to San Cataldo, a little island off the port of Cozze, as a translator for the Libyan workmen. The archaeology team have gone elsewhere. I wasn't told where. In the crypt of a little Renaissance church at the edge of the island's lone village, the Gestapo set the Libyans to work breaking through a wall. The Gestapo had discovered from some old documents that a larger cellar adjoining the crypt had been sealed up centuries before, its memory forgotten by the locals. Their plan was to put the dozens of crates they had brought from North Africa inside this second cellar and seal it back up. I recognized the two attached ammunition boxes among them.

"I directed the labor while the Gestapo kept the villagers away, saying they were setting up a temporary radio transmission station. They even put an antenna on the steeple to add credibility to this story. The Libyans soon broke through to the old cellar, a large vaulted room that was empty except for some rotten old wine barrels, and we placed the boxes inside.

"Once done, what I knew would happen took place. The Gestapo drew their Lugers and gunned down the workmen. As I stood rooted in place with horror they told me that only because I was a loyal party member that I got to live, and that on pain of death I could never divulge what I had seen here. They then sealed up the breach with their own hands and plastered it over so that no one could tell the entrance to the hidden cellar had ever been opened."

The journal had continued until the end of the war when Lieutenant Giordano had surrendered to the Americans. There was no more mention of what happened to the treasure the Gestapo had hidden on the little island of San Cataldo and no indication of what happened to the man who had played a bit part in the drama of the Staff of Ra.

Jana shook Jacob, who lay fast asleep beside her.

"Get up. We need to get going."

Luckily, the village of Cozze opposite the island was only a three-hour drive away.

She hoped they could get there before Dr. Farag and his crew.

CHAPTER FOURTEEN

Dr. Moswen Farag was getting close, he felt sure of it.

On the trip into Italy, he had checked and rechecked his notes, thanking his own caution that he had brought them along with him. Hamza and the others had joked about having to lug boxes of "worthless old papers" all around the Mediterranean, but he had always suspected they might come in handy.

Now they did.

Many years ago, when he had still been an Egyptologist, he had visited Moscow for a conference. The nation was enjoying a brief period of openness. The Soviet Union had fallen years before, and Vladimir Putin hand not yet clenched Russia in his iron grip.

While there, he managed to get into the old Soviet archives, closed to visitors until recently, and searched through captured Nazi documents. He had struggled with the Russians' bad filing system as much as he had with his mediocre German, but he had found what he sought—Gestapo records detailing the evacuation of plunder from the North African Campaign.

The famous lost treasure of Rommel.

Even these once-classified papers of the Nazi secret police had been written in hints, oblique references, and obfuscations. He had spent years teasing out the meanings until he thought he knew where the treasure lay hidden.

And now he was heading for it—a church on the little island of San Cataldo just off the coast from the port of Cozze.

***

In any other circumstances, Jana would have thought the island of San Cataldo idyllic. A green jewel in the Adriatic Sea, it was covered with grass and a few hardy trees. A herd of goats munched grass on a nearby slope. At one end of the island were clustered a few dozen stone houses roofed in red tile, the only settlement on the island. Even coming into the little harbor, she could see the steeple of the church of the saint that gave the island its name.

It stood on the other end of the island, a full mile away from the settlement.

Good. That might help them get this done without arousing suspicion.

"That's the Church of San Cataldo," the sailor who they had hired to take them here said, crossing himself. "He's the patron saint of Taranto. He was an Irish holy man who was sailing back from a pilgrimage to Jerusalem. His ship grounded near Taranto, and the people there convinced him to become their bishop. He was the best bishop the city ever had, a wise and kind man who went all over the countryside preaching. Once he came to this island to preach to the people here, and the people erected the church in his honor. That was back in the Middle Ages. That church was made later, in the sixteenth century."

“You know a lot about local history,” Jana said.

The man laughed. “You mean I know a lot for a sailor. All the people here know the stories of San Cataldo.”

“Are there services today?”

“Just evening mass. You should have come on a Sunday. The whole island shows up. Don’t worry, the church is always open.”

Good. I don’t want Jacob picking the lock to the church door. That probably counts as a sin.

“I’m looking forward to seeing it,” Jana said in a massive understatement.

Because the old shiver of anticipation had come back to her, the exquisite thrill of knowing you were on the cusp of a discovery. Like when one of her workers uncovered the first spot on that Roman mosaic in Morocco, or when they clambered down a sea cave on the Caribbean coast and their flashlights caught a first glimpse of that wonderfully preserved pirate ship.

They were about to see something that no one had seen for eighty years—the lost treasure of General Erwin Rommel.

She stared at the island as the sailor brought his motorboat into the little cove that was the island’s lone harbor. A few other motorboats and small fishing vessels took up most of the spaces in the pier. A couple of larger yachts were moored a bit further out, too big for this humble port. Jana guessed they were owned by wealthy vacationers taking pleasure cruises around the Adriatic Sea.

She looked back toward the church of San Cataldo, now disappearing behind a rise in the terrain. To think that that little church hid such a big secret …

The sailor's laugh brought he out of her reverie.

"You're not going to get much use out of that motorcycle," he said, jabbing a thumb toward the motorbike Jacob had rented. It was lashed to the stern of the boat. A pair of leather saddlebags held their weapons and some tools. "You can circle the whole island with that in twenty minutes."

Jana only smiled. How could she explain to this friendly local that Jacob always tried to have access to a speedy getaway?

They docked. Jacob and the sailor struggled to get the motorcycle off the boat and onto the pier, helped by a bored local teen who asked for a ride in broken English.

"Sorry, kid," Jacob said. "Maybe later."

The kid shrugged and went back to his fishing pole.

They wheeled the bike into a town that couldn't have housed more than three hundred people, revved it up, and set off. Jana felt nervous, seeing all eyes upon her. Two old men playing backgammon in front of the town's lone cafe looked up from their game. A pair of fishermen unloading their catch stopped too. The woman hanging her washing stopped and leaned against the windowsill, not even trying to hide the fact that she was watching them.

A small hotel by the pier showed that tourists occasionally came here, but she suspected so little happened on this island that everyone stared at strangers.

They certainly were staring at her and Jacob. A little too much, she thought.

In less than a minute, they sped out of town and down a narrow road that hugged the shoreline. It hadn't been repaved in a while, and the motorcycle bumped over poorly sealed cracks and several potholes. Other than a couple of lonesome cottages and a man tending a herd of goats, they saw no one.

Jana, sitting behind Jacob with her arms wrapped around his middle, breathed in the fresh sea air and felt her heart race.

She and Jacob were about to make another amazing discovery, and this time there was no one around to ruin it. Finally, they could win one without any accompanying disasters.

The road swung around the curved shore of the island and then cut up over a low hill and straight on to the church, which stood close to the edge of a steep slope leading down to the shore. She saw the road continued around the other side of the island, presumably back to town. One circular road was all the little island of San Cataldo could justify.

The stone church was a humble one, small and with a plain whitewashed facade and a short bell tower barely rising above the gabled roof. A pair of wooden doors with iron fittings stood closed.

Jacob parked the motorcycle in the dirt lot in front of the church, grabbed the saddlebags, and they dismounted. To her relief, they found the doors unlocked just as the sailor said they'd be.

They opened them with a creak and stood in the doorway, trying to adjust their eyes after the brilliant sunshine reflecting off the water.

There was little illumination inside except what came through a small stained glass window above the altar, showing San Cataldo in a red robe with his mitre and crozier, looking down on a miniature version of the island that bore his name.

A few candles burned by the altar. An old woman, dressed all in black, was lighting one. She didn't look back at them but simply bowed her head and started praying in low tones. They entered, taking a last look outside to make sure no one else was around, then closed the door behind them.

Together they walked quietly down the aisle, glancing at the twelve stations of the cross marked around the interior wall. Jana admired a few old paintings that hung here, somber oils showing various saints and the holy family. She spotted a small doorway to the right of the altar, half hidden by a faded red curtain. Jana elbowed Jacob and nodded in that direction.

He stopped, staring at the stained glass window. Jana did the same.

It took a couple of minutes, but their patience was rewarded. The woman finished praying, crossed herself, and left.

As soon as the door thudded shut behind her, they made a beeline to the smaller door near the altar.

It was unlocked, and opened onto darkness.

Jana fumbled around, found a light switch just inside the door, and turned it on. A single bare bulb illuminated an arched passageway with worn steps leading down. The air felt damp and cool.

Together they went downstairs and found themselves in a small crypt with flagstone graves marked with the names and dates of past priests and local notables, some dating back centuries. A small church with a long history.

It had more history than most people suspected.

Jana scanned the walls, painted white with plaster. Whoever had hidden the passageway to the other cellar had done a good job. She couldn't see any irregularities anywhere. Plus, given the freshness of the plaster, it looked like it got a new coat regularly.

The stairway had curved to the left, so now they faced a different direction from when they started. That meant the wall to the right of the end of the stairs was in the direction of a steep slope behind the church. No room for a large chamber there. The wall with the stairway probably didn't hold a chamber either since the stairway itself cut through the center of the space. To her left was the space directly beneath the church, and unlikely location for an earlier cellar that had escaped notice during the initial construction.

Only the wall directly in front of her remained as a likely candidate.

Jana walked over to it and, starting at one end of the wall and moving toward the other, ran her hands up and down along the plaster.

About a third of the way along, the wall turned from smooth stones to having a few slight ripples to it. She moved her hands around, tracing the almost undetectable bumps. They made rectangles. A series of rectangles.

Bricks and mortar.

"Here," Jana said, her voice loud in the crypt. "It's here."

Jacob opened the bags and pulled out a pair of chisels, another pair of picks, and two mallets.

They got to work. The secret they had been searching for lay just beyond this brick wall.

CHAPTER FIFTEEN

Jacob wiped his brow as he hacked away at the bricks. They had removed several coats of plaster to reveal a bricked-up space just big enough to allow a man to pass through, and now they were chiseling away at the mortar connecting them. He sure hoped no one had come to visit the church because they were making a hell of a racket.

With a crash, a chunk of brickwork fell away to leave a dark hole. After that it became easier, Jacob and Jana working away at the jagged edges to bring more bricks down until they had a space big enough to step through at a crouch.

Before they did, Jana turned on a flashlight she had brought along, her face eager with anticipation.

She deserves this, he thought with a smile.

That smile faded at the look of confusion on her face, quickly replaced with shock.

Jacob peered through the hole and jerked with surprise.

A large vaulted chamber stood entirely empty save for a single box without a lid sitting in the middle of the floor.

Jana stepped through the hole and Jacob followed, first grabbing his MP5. He didn't like to go anywhere unarmed, not even church.

They approached the box and peered inside. A note lay at the bottom on yellowed paper. A couple of lines in Italian were written on it.

Jana picked it up and read, "Got here first, 3 December, 1973. Too bad for you."

"Damn it!" Jana shouted. "We were so close! Now what the hell do we do?"

She kicked the box, swore as it hurt her foot, then kicked it again. Jacob wandered around the room. That couldn't be it, could it? Maybe there was another hidden door somewhere.

As Jana stomped around the chamber, shouting words he had never heard her use (and a lot of them), Jacob made a slow survey of the room.

He was in a far corner of the same wall where the opening was when a man's voice spoke.

"Jana Peters, how good to see you again."

Jacob froze. Jana whirled around and shone her flashlight at the entrance, leaving Jacob in the shadows. He stayed where he was, invisible for the moment.

A hulking man who looked Egyptian stepped through the hole, leveling a pump-action shotgun at her. Jacob raised his MP5 and hesitated. If he shot this guy, his finger might squeeze the trigger and take out Jana. No way he'd miss with a shotgun at this range.

Another young Egyptian stepped through the hole, and another. Both carried automatic pistols. Jacob edged along the wall, sticking to the shadows. The terrorists glanced round, but there was no light to see him by and their eyes passed right over his position.

Then the man he knew he'd see stepped through the hole.

Dr. Farag.

"I must admit, Ms. Peters, that I'm disappointed you found this before me, although it's not nearly as disappointing as finding it empty."

Jacob took a final couple of steps and placed the muzzle of his MP5 against Dr. Farag's temple.

"Not as disappointed as you're going to feel when your brains get spattered all across the floor."

The former Egyptologist froze.

The big guy growled in broken English, "You kill him, we kill the bitch."

"She prefers the term Professor Peters," Jacob replied.

One of the others began to turn toward him.

"Don't move. Any more guns trained on me and your leader gets it. Then you'll never find the Staff of Ra."

Will we ever find it?

For a moment, no one spoke.

"This is pointless," Jana said. "If anyone fires, most of us will die. Maybe all of us. I propose a truce. We ease back and walk out of here."

Pause.

"It's a trick," the big guy told his boss in Arabic. "Let's kill her."

"And what do you think will happen to me, Hamza?" Dr. Farag said with the patient tone one uses for a slow child.

"We can't let them go. We're already racing against the Libyans."

Dr. Farag winced.

The Libyans?

Even Hamza realized he had said too much. He bit his lip, brow furrowing.

"Jana's right," Jacob said. "You shoot her, I shoot you, and then try to take out the other three. I shoot you, they shoot her and probably me. Lose-lose either way."

Dr. Farag nodded. "I see the reasoning. Much as I hate to say it, I think you're right. Very well. We'll step out of the chamber first and—"

Jacob interrupted him. "Not on your life. We're outnumbered. We go first."

"I don't think so," Hamza said.

"Look," Jana said. "Dr. Farag goes out with Jacob right behind. He's too slow to duck to the side and get out of the line of fire."

"Thank you," Dr. Farag said.

"It's true. You should hit the gym. Anyway. They go out first, then Hamza goes out with me. The other two stay here. That way it's even. Then we go up the stairs, and me and Jacob slip out the door. We close it and run. You guys wait a couple of minutes until we're gone.

No way they'll wait a couple of minutes. We'll end up in a gunfight in the damn church. At least we'll be out of this Mexican standoff.

"Very well," Dr. Farag said.

Jacob nudged him with his gun. "Let's go, and don't try to prove Jana wrong about your physical fitness."

"I have no wish to be martyred until my work on Earth is complete."

"And what would that be?"

"You'll see soon enough."

Not if I can help it.

Dr. Farag stepped through the hole, Jacob keeping his MP5 pressed to his skull. Then Jacob went through. They stood at the far end of the crypt as Jana passed through the hole, Hamza right behind her.

"All right," Jacob announced. "You two in there, stay put like good little boys. We're going to walk up the stairs, slowly and calmly, and then me and Jana will pass through the door."

Hamza and Dr. Farag traded a look.

"Don't get eager for those 72 virgins," Jacob told them. "I even up the odds because I can take out the both of you."

"And lose your slut," Hamza said.

"You're much more eloquent in Arabic," Jacob replied. "I might just have to kill your boss out of a sense of outraged feminism."

"Shut up, Jacob," Jana said.

"Fine. Take his side."

They moved cautiously up the stairs, each gunman following his hostage.

"So Dawson's staff was a fake, eh?" Jacob said.

"Obviously, or I wouldn't be here," Dr. Farag grumbled.

When they got to the top, Jacob ordered Dr. Farag to stop.

"I'll get the door. Don't want you slamming it in my face and leaving us alone with Herman Munster here."

Keeping his gun pressed between the Egyptologist's eyes, he eased open the door and stepped out.

"OK, Jana. You next."

Jana squeezed past him.

"Remember, you give us two minutes."

"We will keep our side of the bargain."

Yeah, right.

He slammed the door in their face and leapt out of the way. Jana had already gotten out of the line of fire. Smart woman.

To his surprise, no gunfire erupted through the door. He and Jana raced down the aisle.

Still no shots. Did they suspect a trap and were taking it slow?

He felt tempted to go back and finish them off, but he was outnumbered, and they only had one gun with one magazine. The rest were in the saddlebags back with the terrorists.

They ran out to the motorcycle and were surprised to see no other vehicles here. Had the terrorists walked?

Good. That meant they could get to the docks well before them, grab someone with a boat, and get the hell off this island.

Jacob gunned the engine, and they sped off. Just as they did, Jana shouted in his ear,

"They're coming out of the church!"

Both ducked. Several shots crackled in the distance, but no bullets found them. In another second, they were down the slope and out of sight.

The road curved along the shore. Jacob laughed.

"Dumbasses! They walked to the church. Now they're way behind."

"Um, Jacob … "

Something in her tone made him look over his shoulder. Four motorcycles were gaining on them. Hamza drove in front with another of the terrorists. The third terrorist was close behind, with Dr. Farag staying safely in the rear.

Hamza and the other terrorist in front drove with one hand, aiming at them with pistols.

"Crap! No fair hiding their bikes!"

They fired. Jacob swerved, and the bullets went wild. He put on some speed, pushing the undersized rental to its limit. The terrorists kept on their tail.

More shots Jacob kept swerving. It was hard to fire from a moving platform at a moving target, but sooner or later they were going to hit. He had to do something. Fast.

Then he saw another problem. As the road curved around a tight bend, he spotted a group of kids playing soccer right on the road. There was so little traffic on this island that was something you could do safely.

Except when there was a high-speed chase involving gunfire.

The kids were already parting for them, but that didn't matter. He wouldn't put it past Hamza and his crew to gun them down as they passed.

Jacob spotted a faint trail leading up the slope, perhaps one used by the herdsmen he'd spotted at various spots on the island. He turned and got onto that, the motorcycle bumping and juddering over the rocky path. Jana tightened her grip around his middle. They had only made it a few yards when a bullet punched a hole in the edge of his windshield.

He flinched, nearly lost control, and regained it. Jacob and Jana both kept low as they moved up the hill.

No more shots came. Jacob didn't dare take a look over his shoulder—he couldn't take his eyes off the rough path for an instant—but he figured the terrorists were still following. No way to drive one-handed and shoot on this terrain.

Up the crest of the hill and down the other side. The path got even rougher. Jacob prayed they didn't get a flat tire.

The island was narrower than it was long, and soon they made it to the road on the other side. As they got on the pavement, Jacob dared a glance and saw the terrorists lagging behind, and he didn't see Dr. Farag at all.

Probably had a spill. Hope he broke his damn neck. Probably not, though, knowing my luck.

Jacob picked up speed and soon looped around the island and spotted the village.

Only to get stopped short by a herd of goats, of all things.

They took up the whole road, and the slope was too steep in this section for him to go around. Jacob cursed, slowed, and the goats slowly parted, bleating in protest as he bumped through them. The goatherd, an older Italian man in a broadbrimmed hat and faded canvas pants, shouted at him.

"Sorry to disturb your goats, sir, but I'm being chased by terrorists. You might want to make yourself scarce."

He said this in English, and the man only stared at him dumbly. The Italian looked down the road, and his eyes widened.

"They're gaining on us!" Jana shouted. The goatherd scrambled down the slope and out of the way.

Jacob gunned it, getting past the last of the goats, which now hugged either side of the road.

Giving a clear path for the terrorists.

They zoomed in after Jacob and Jana and started firing again.

That got stopped as soon as they got into the winding streets of the village. Jacob prayed they wouldn't come across any bystanders.

Luckily no one was on the streets, and the village was so small than he passed through it in less than a minute, coming to the pier.

The bored teen was still fishing off the pier. He turned to look with excitement as he heard the roar of the motorcycle …

… then dove into the water as bullets started to fly.

Jacob had no time to stop, no time to get a boat, and he had run out of places to go. Another loop around the island to try and shake them would more likely end up in them or one of the islanders getting killed.

He looked at the two yachts moored not far off the pier and got an idea.

"Hang on!" Jacob shouted.

Jacob revved the motorcycle and shot at full speed down the pier. A coil of rope sat right at the end. Perfect.

He pulled up on the bike, hit the coil of rope at full speed, and sailed in a high arc over the water. He hoped that teenager got to see.

Only when Jacob reached the top of his parabola did he realize that he was never going to make it to the nearest yacht.

The motorcycle began its inevitable descent. Jacob and Jana let go and hit the water with a hard splash.

CHAPTER SIXTEEN

Jana sputtered and coughed as she came to the surface. She wiped her eyes, spotted the yacht only a few yards away, and swam for it, Jacob at her side. A couple of bullets splashed in the water nearby. They swam around to the far side of the yacht for cover and clambered aboard.

I hope no one's on board. This would be hard to explain.

Someone was.

A sleepy-eyed Egyptian man came up from below, looking confused. As he spotted them, he grabbed a marlinspike, murder in his eyes. Jacob ducked his swing and took him out with a karate chop to the neck, beat his head against the deck until he was dead, and tossed him overboard.

"We're in their boat!" Jana said.

"I guess that's why they stopped shooting at us."

Jacob went to the helm and started up the yacht while Jana retrieved the anchor. She spotted the Egyptians piling into the same motor launch that had brought her and Jacob to the island. The teenaged fisherman was swimming away from the scene, his boredom replaced by terror.

Jacob revved up the engine, which sounded powerful, and took off, soon leaving the terrorists behind.

"We need to go into hiding," he said over the roar of the engine. "They'll keep after us. I can't believe that damn crypt was empty. The Staff of Ra could be anywhere. Does that diary you stole from Garibaldi have any more clues?"

Jana gasped. The diary! It had been in her pocket the whole time.

She pulled it out of her soaked pocket, water dripping from it. Gritting her teeth, she opened it up.

Only to find the ink had run into an illegible smear.

***

Aaron Peters had come to Taranto thinking he'd find Jacob and Jana, and found Mort Wheeler instead.

Wheeler had been fresh out of training the year Aaron went into his long undercover operation in the Middle East. He had never known the kid well, but Aaron never forgot a face.

Even though Wheeler was ten years older now and had grown a beard.

Aaron wasn't surprised to see him here. He had risked exposing himself by calling the CIA for reinforcements. They were bound to send someone, he just hadn't known that Wheeler had been assigned to the European sector.

What he did know was that Wheeler was tailing someone. It was obvious.

Well, not obvious to the guys he was tailing, but obvious to him from his vantage point half a block behind Wheeler.

Aaron couldn't get a good look at the three men Wheeler was after because of the twists and turns of the Italian streets, just that they were all young and fit Europeans and wearing the overly loud clothing of tourists, a perfect way to blend in when you're doing ops in a touristy place like this.

Except this neighborhood wasn't touristy. It was a back street with a few little shops in the ground floors of apartment buildings, well away from the port and the castle and the museums.

They came to a straighter road, and he got a good view of the trio for the first time. They were looking around a bit more now, as if close to their destination. They looked right at Wheeler but didn't focus on him, and they barely registered Aaron. It was just after work and lot of people were walking home or heading out for a coffee or wine at one of the town's many cafes. Cars and the occasional delivery truck passed by in the street. It was easy to blend in, especially for trained men like Mort Wheeler and Aaron Peters.

Two of the men entered a shop, while the third stood outside and lit a cigarette. Wheeler ducked into a bakery with a large window that would allow him to keep an eye on the target while the glare of the sun made it impossible for the smoker to see him.

Aaron slowed his pace to give himself maximum time to see what was going on.

The smoker was looking all around, but didn't seem to detect danger, only stay on the alert for it. Just above his head hung a sign reading, "Taranto Books: New, Used, and Rare."

Aaron passed by the bakery, hoping Wheeler didn't recognize him. He'd aged a lot in the past ten years and wore a baseball cap low over his face. He also turned his face away from the bakery window as he passed.

He wished he could reach out to Wheeler, but he couldn't trust him. Aaron couldn't trust anyone in the CIA. It was a terrible thing to look into the faces of your colleagues and wonder what evil might lie behind them. Aaron felt like some close relative had just been found guilty of a major crime. It made him question all his presuppositions and left him feeling paranoid and very, very alone.

It also made him feel vulnerable. Calling in the potential hit on Jacob and Jana had exposed himself, and if the mole or moles caught wind of it, it wouldn't take much reasoning to deduce that he'd show up in Taranto.

The main thing right now was to find out who Wheeler was following and if this was the "cleanup team" Jacob had called in a warning about.

He also had to wonder if there was a cleanup team gunning for him too.

A tobacconist's stood two doors down from the bookshop, and that gave him an idea. As he came opposite the bookshop, with the lookout giving him a once-over, Aaron glanced both ways to check for traffic and crossed the street at an angle to get to the tobacconist's, feeling the lookout's eyes on him.

Aaron resisted the urge to look right at the bookshop. From his peripheral vision, he could tell no one was visible through the window, which was full of books that obscured the view.

Without looking back, he entered the tobacconist's. A young Italian woman was just leaving, and he went up to the counter to buy a pack of cigarettes.

Not that he planned to smoke them. He had enough unhealthy habits already.

He took his time paying and then lingered in the shop a minute, pretending to examine some cigars while monitoring the street through the glass door.

This tactic got rewarded when he saw the three men pass by. The lookout glanced at the shop interior through the glass door, but by then Aaron had already half turned away.

He counted to five and left the shop.

Just in time to see Wheeler cross the street from the bakery and enter the bookshop. The three men were just turning a corner and going out of sight.

Aaron was about to follow when Wheeler came out, looking worried.

Aaron knew that look all too well. It meant whoever was inside was dead. Wheeler certainly hadn't had time to question anyone alive in there.

As the younger agent got on the phone, Aaron moved off and rounded the same corner the trio had gone around.

He spotted them at the end of a side street that opened onto a major thoroughfare.

Good. Lots of traffic and lots of people. He could tail these guys easily.

And tail them he would. Now he knew this was the cleanup team sent by The Order. Why they'd hit someone in a bookshop wasn't clear to him, but the CIA was monitoring them and so would he.

Because these guys must be on the trail of Jacob and Jana. Since he had no idea where they had gotten to, he would tail these guys until they led him to his daughter and his old student.

He just hoped he could head them off before they attacked.

***

Jana sat glumly in their hotel room about fifty miles down the coast from Cozze and the island of San Cataldo. Outside, tourists were enjoying the sunset, sipping wine in the cafes or strolling along a brilliant beach and admiring the azure water as the sun slanted low in the west.

She wasn't in the mood for any of that. The Staff of Ra was nowhere to be found, the journal was destroyed, and they were all out of leads.

Her only hope was a laptop Jacob had retrieved from the yacht, along with a cache of weapons and a large wad of cash. That gave them the resources to keep hunting, and left The Sword of the Righteous with fewer resources.

Jacob hoped to hack into the laptop.

Once they had sailed to Cozze, they had made a beeline to their rental car and sped off here before the pursuing terrorists could see where they were going. Luckily in the trunk Jacob had a sophisticated CIA computer that he could connect to the Egyptian laptop. Now, he was running a program to break through the encryption.

It was taking some time. Dr. Farag had invested in good protection. That made Jana all the more interested in seeing what was on it.

Jana paced, becoming increasingly impatient. Those Libyans Hamza mentioned were way ahead of them. They could have found Rommel's treasure already. It twisted her gut to think that not one but two different Islamist groups wanted to build a nuclear device.

Jacob could probably rattle off the names of twenty more. What an ugly world he lived in.

And now she had to live in it too.

But in fact, she reasoned, everybody lived in that world. They just weren't aware of it.

She couldn't decide whether to envy them or pity those innocent civilians. Maybe a bit of both.

"Got it!" Jacob announced.

She was across the room and looking over his shoulder in a heartbeat.

CHAPTER SEVENTEEN

Jacob gave Jana a kiss. Nothing like hacking into a terrorist's computer to cheer up his girl.

The wallpaper of Dr. Farag's laptop showed an image of the Dome of the Rock, the golden-domed mosque built atop the ancient Temple of Solomon in Jerusalem. It was the third holiest place in Islam and a rallying point for Islamists who wanted to push the Jews out of the region.

Several folders were labeled "Research 1, Research 2, Research 3 …"

Jacob clicked on "Research 1" and came up with a bunch of image files without thumbnails.

"You might not want to look at this stuff," Jacob said.

He didn't want to either. He'd seen plenty of Islamist torture and execution images. They were seared into his brain and could never be removed. He wanted to spare Jana that, even though she'd seen far more than her share of bloodshed.

Hopefully, they'll be something more useful than that. Maps, maybe?

"I'm not looking," Jana told him.

Jacob clicked on the first image and was greeted by a smiling naked Thai woman spreading her legs.

Jacob laughed. "Oh, Dr. Farag. You are a naughty boy!"

"What?" Jana asked.

He clicked on another image and saw another naked Thai woman in a suggestive pose.

"I sense a trend," Jacob muttered. He clicked on a third image and was treated to more bare Asian flesh.

"Hmm. At least he has good taste in something."

A slap upside the head told him Jana had finally looked at the screen.

"Stop messing around. We have a world to save!"

"I'm gathering intel. Delving into the innermost thoughts of a terrorist mastermind."

"You're acting like a teenaged boy."

“I’m young at heart. What can I say?”

“Stop being annoying and find something useful.”

“Sheesh. All right, all right.”

He clicked on the folder labeled "Research 2."

There he found a series of Word documents with labels such as “Corsica”, “Malta”, and “San Cataldo.”

“Now we’re getting somewhere,” Jana said.

“We still haven’t made an adequate survey of the first folder.”

“Stop acting like a high schooler and open that file on Corsica. I seem to remember hearing a rumor that Rommel’s treasure was buried there. Something I saw on some bogus TV documentary.”

The document was hard to read. Not that it was in Arabic, which both of them read fluently, but because it contained nothing more than a series of Dr. Farag’s notes to himself, mostly brief phrases such as “southeast coast near marina?”, “POW camp story not true,” and, “buried or simply submerged?”

Jana groaned. They went through the other documents and found them all similar. The rogue Egyptologist obviously had another set of notes somewhere, perhaps in hard copy, and these notes referred to those. Perhaps they had been secreted in that yacht they stole but never had time to search.

No way they could go back to the Cozze marina. Not only would the terrorists be waiting, but the cops would like to have a word with them too.

One document was labelled “San Cataldo.” Judging from the notes, this was Dr. Farag’s first choice. At least they could scratch that off the list. It was difficult to see which other potential hiding place Dr. Farag favored after that one.

But it did tell them one thing—Dr. Farag would have visited San Cataldo first. The other sites hadn’t been searched yet.

At least not by him. But by the Libyans? Hard to say since he had no idea how far their research had gone, and down what avenues. All he knew was that he and Jana needed to figure out the most likely spot now before the Libyans made it there.

Because he had to assume the Staff of Ra hadn’t been stolen back in 1973 by whoever had left that mocking note. If the staff had been in that crypt, it would surely have surfaced in the intervening fifty years. Dr. Farag or Dawson or someone else would have gotten a hold of it.

So Rommel’s treasure was still out there—hidden and waiting to unleash a terrible crime upon the world.

Jacob turned to his partner. "We need to do some serious research, and fast. We haven't really had time to delve into all the rumors and conspiracy theories because we had solid leads. Now we're going to have to if we want a chance to figure out which of these spots is the most likely."

Jana nodded. "I'll get to it."

"We'll get to it. This is way more your specialty than mine, but we don't have much time. We might not have any time at all. We'll each work on one location, then move on to the next. We'll dredge up whatever we can online. Know any specialists we can call?"

"Hard to say until we've dug through the material here."

"All right. Let's get to it and figure out what we can."

***

Six hours later, Jana rubbed her eyes and suppressed a yawn. It was approaching midnight and other than ordering some room service, they hadn't budged from their laptops. It had been a grueling, mostly fruitless search through a mass of wild speculation, half-baked history, and outright conspiracy theories.

Mostly fruitless, but not entirely.

Because they had narrowed the search down to three likely suspects.

Assuming Rommel's treasure hadn't been sent on a UFO to a Nazi moon base like one Internet theory held.

Dismissing that as unlikely (although after all Jana seen lately she couldn't dismiss anything) the three main prospects were Corsica, La Isla Perejil off the Moroccan coast, and the island of Giannutri off the western coast of Italy near the town of Grosseto in Tuscany, about a two hour drive north of Rome.

Dr. Farag had listed five other possibilities, but for various reasons, not always clear from his notes, he had dismissed them as serious candidates.

Corsica seemed to be the more favored theory among researchers who didn't hold totally outlandish views. The story was based on testimony by one Peter Fleig, an SS diver who claimed that in 1943 he was ordered by a group of SS officers to hide six ammunition boxes in an undersea cave just off the east coast of Corsica, which was then still under Nazi control.

He and the officers then fled to Italy but fell into Allied hands. Fleig said the Allies knew they had hidden a treasure and tried to get them to reveal its location. The officers, loyal to Hitler to the last, refused and were executed. Fleig managed to pretend ignorance, convincing his captors that he was a simple soldier who had fallen in with the officers and didn't know anything about any treasure.

Another SS soldier, Corporal Walter Kimer, ended his war in Dachau, the notorious concentration camp. The Americans had converted it into a POW camp for suspected war criminals and members of the SS. Being such a low rank, Kimer was soon released. While he returned to obscurity, rumors circulated after his death that he had learned the location of the hidden sea cave from Fleig or someone else during his imprisonment. An investigator unearthed an old photo of him in his uniform that had a code on the back the investigator believed to be the coordinates to the cave. This code was never made public, and the investigator never found the cave.

Jana noted that this part of the story was labeled "untrue" by Dr. Farag, for reasons he didn't put down in the computer file.

Fleig reappeared in Corsica in 1948, hiring some local fishermen to take him out on a boat to a spot near the port of Bastia to search of the cave. They made several trips but couldn't find it. The local Mafia, figuring that a former German soldier snooping around the waters off their city might signify something, began to get interested. Fleig disappeared, never to be heard from again.

In later years, the two fishermen who he hired took several teams out to the area where Fleig reportedly searched, but nothing was ever found.

La Isla Perejil, which in Spanish means "parsley island", is a small, uninhabited island, little more than an oversized rock, just off the coast of Morocco. It is claimed by Spain and was the subject of controversy over the years because the Moroccans said that Spanish control was a legacy of colonialism and wanted it back. They also demanded the ports of Ceuta and Melilla, two Spanish exclaves on the Moroccan coast.

The little island was the flashpoint of an international incident in 2002 when Morocco sent soldiers to the island, who erected a Moroccan flag and started setting up a base there.

After much fulminating, the Spanish sent an overwhelming force of naval ships and commandos. The small group of Moroccan troops did the smart thing and surrendered, were quickly repatriated, and after a long negotiation, things went back to the way they were before.

The link with Rommel's treasure is a story emerging from a little-known Spanish book published anonymously in 1960 titled *El Oro de Rommel*, "The Gold of Rommel." In it, the author quotes various German and Spanish veterans who were involved in shipping the treasure from Tunisia first to Barcelona in Spain, which was then controlled by the Fascist dictator Francisco Franco. Franco, while broadly supporting Hitler, had kept his country out of the war because it was exhausted from a bitter civil war that had only ended in 1939.

The treasure was kept in a bank vault in Barcelona until 1944. It was supposed to go direct to Berlin, but there were delays because of a dispute among the German high command as to what should be done with it. Some felt it should continue on to Berlin as soon as possible, while others said it was safer in a neutral country.

In the end, part of the treasure got liquidated in Spain in exchange for shipments of Spanish agricultural and manufactured goods to Germany, whose economy was feeling the strain from five years of war and bombardment.

Then in early 1945, with Germany increasingly isolated and losing territory, Berlin sent the order through its embassy in Madrid to move the material out of Spain. Hitler feared that soon the Allies would turn their sights on Fascist Spain, an invasion that in the end never happened.

It was decided to hide the remaining boxes, which included "jewelry and precious antiquities," in northern Morocco, which was then a Spanish colony. The book gives accounts from three soldiers—two Spanish and one German—who were in the party that went to Isla Perejil and buried the boxes in a deep shaft they had excavated. After the war, the two Spanish soldiers tried to return but were barred from overseas travel for life. Similarly, when the German soldier tried to return, he was denied a visa to Spanish Morocco. The Spanish government obviously had a list of everyone associated with the mission and would not let them anywhere near the island.

The third possibility was the island of Giannutri off the Tuscan coast. This story was basically a variation of the Corsica theory, except that it was a different group of soldiers led by Obersturmführer Gunther Weiss, a member of both the SS and the Gestapo, the feared German secret police.

Weiss was ordered to accompany the treasure to Taranto, where it was loaded onto trucks to be driven north through Italy and into Germany. The five soldiers with him had no idea what the boxes contained or what Obersturmführer Weiss's orders were.

This gave the Gestapo man an idea. He asked for a detailed map of Italy from the general in command in Taranto, saying that due to partisan activity and heavy Allied bombing, he might need to change his route at any minute. Once he got that map, he studied it in great detail and came up with a plan that was very different than the one had had been given.

He ordered his men to drive north, appearing to follow his orders to go to Germany. But when he got about two-thirds of the way up the peninsula, he had his men head to the coast, secure a boat, and they sailed to the island of Giannutri.

The soldiers didn't question this sudden detour. They thought it was all part of the plan.

Obersturmführer Weiss had studied geology in university and saw that Giannutri was mostly made up of limestone, which often forms caves, especially when exposed to rain and the sea. His idea was to hide the treasure in one of these caves.

The team searched the island for several days before he found the best place for it, a small cave with an entrance that remained underwater even at low tide. The team had to swim in pairs, hauling the heavy boxes as far as they could before swimming back, gulping in some air, and then diving underwater again to get the boxes a few feet further in.

It was a grueling task, and one man died in the effort.

When they were all finished and the boxes were secure in the dry portion of the cave, the soldiers lay on the nearby beach, utterly exhausted. Obersturmführer Weiss pulled out his Luger and gunned them down.

This story was related by Captain Dwight Mitchell of the U.S. Marine Corps, who captured Obersturmführer Weiss during the Italian campaign a year later.

Being a member of both the Gestapo and the SS, Weiss feared he would be tried and executed and offered his story to Mitchell in exchange for his freedom.

Mitchell listened carefully to the story, asking for as much detail as possible, and then shot the Nazi in cold blood.

After the war, Mitchell made numerous trips to the island, but could never locate the treasure.

“So what do you think?” Jacob asked, standing and stretching. He'd been hunched over a laptop for hours, just like her.

"I don't know," Jana admitted. "Each of these stories is vague, with a lot of hints and suppositions. If we didn't know the Staff of Ra actually exists, I wouldn’t believe any of them.”

“Well, which do you believe is the most likely?”

Jana let out a long sigh and rubbed her temples. “I don’t know. None stands out from the others.”

“Well, we got to narrow it down somehow. We can’t be in three places at the same time!”

Jana thought for a moment.

“I don’t know what to tell you. But I do know someone who might be able to narrow it down.”

CHAPTER EIGHTEEN

Jana hadn't spoken to Professor Luis Abascal for a couple of years. He was a retired Spanish historian and archaeologist who specialized in the colonial period of Morocco. So while their regions had been the same, their research interests hadn't overlapped. Still, he had been an amiable older gentleman who was always a lively mainstay at any broad-based academic conference on Morocco's past.

He had also written a book about the Spanish colony of northern Morocco during the Second World War.

Jana looked him up and gave him a call at his home in Cadiz.

After some initial pleasantries and catching up, during which Jana tried not to show her impatience, she got down to business.

"I'm working on a popular level article about archaeological mysteries in Morocco and I wonder what you think of the theory of Rommel's treasure being located on La Isla Perejil." She made her tone sound jocular, as if she couldn't believe such an outlandish tale.

Dr. Abascal chuckled. "My, my, as if that wonderful mosaic wasn't enough for you, Dr. Peters, and now you are chasing treasure! Well, the story isn't as ridiculous as it sounds. We do know that an SS unit attached to Rommel's army did loot the prosperous Jewish communities of Tunisia and Libya, and they did loot some archaeological sites. So there was, indeed, a treasure."

"Have you read *El Oro de Rommel*?"

She wished she had. She hadn't even heard of the book until a few hours ago.

"I skimmed it many years ago. Full of inconsistencies and suppositions."

"Hm, I see. But I suppose all of these stories are."

"Yes, but there are a couple of key elements to the story that don't ring true. Firstly, La Isla Perejil has long been used by shepherds to graze their flocks. It has a fair amount of grass since the region gets a lot of rain, and so shepherds from the mainland bring sheep or goats over by boat, and then they can just leave them there alone for a time before returning to pick them up. They still do that today."

“So the shepherds would notice any foreigners going to the island and would spot any recent signs of digging.”

“It would certainly be a risk. There are many remote places in northern Morocco, especially in those days, so why go somewhere you might be spotted?”

“Interesting. What’s your other objection?”

“The timing. That book says the German high command feared bringing the treasure back to Germany in 1943. While it certainly would have been a dangerous journey, once it was in Spain it would have been safe. Small items like jewels and gold ingots could have been smuggled in a series of diplomatic pouches to Germany. Also, why go to Morocco at all? If Spain feared an invasion, there are many rural areas in southern Spain that are all but uninhabited. It would have been much easier to bury it on home soil. Yes, Franco feared an invasion, but that would have encompassed its overseas colonies as well. It would have been easier and no more dangerous to bury it in Spain.”

“I see.”

“But there is a final nail in the coffin. When our troops retook La Isla Perejil in 2002, our military engineers probed the island with subsurface imagery to make sure the Moroccans hadn’t built any underground bunkers or traps. I myself got to see the results because I was interested to see if there were any archaeological remains there. They didn’t find anything. While their work wasn’t exhaustive and they might have missed something, it was comprehensive enough that I can say with 99 percent certainty that there is nothing buried on that island.”

"Well, thank you, Dr. Abascal. This has been very helpful."

“Good luck with your article and feel free to call me any time. If you find yourself in Cadiz, we can go out for some tapas and wine.”

“I’d love that. Goodbye.”

“Goodbye.”

Jana turned to Jacob. “We can strike La Isla Perejil off the list.”

“What about Corsica and Giannutri?”

Jana shrugged. “No idea. And I don’t see how we can figure out which is the more likely candidate without weeks if not months of research. What do you think?”

Jacob pulled out a euro coin.

“Heads we go to Corsica, tails we go to Giannutri.”

Jana blinked. “You’re going to flip a coin?”

"Do you have a better idea?"

"You're going to leave the fate of the free world on the balance of a coin toss?"

"You said we have two main options, and we have no way to tell which is the better one. So I repeat, do you have a better idea?"

Jana thought for a moment.

"No, I don't. But to leave this decision to a—"

Jacob tossed the coin.

"Tails. Pack your things. We're going to Giannutri."

The town of Grosseto looked sleepy in the early morning light. Driving through its quiet streets, Jacob saw only a couple of street cleaners and an old woman walking her dog. It was six in the morning, and Jacob needed a coffee. Maybe three coffees. After grinding through all that research, they had to drive seven hours to get here, crossing half the length of Italy.

Grosseto was just 14 kilometers from the shore of the Tyrrhenian Sea off the west coast of Italy, and Jacob had been hoping to find a travel agent offering boat rides here. Nothing looked open, though. Maybe he'd have better luck at the coast.

Just as he was heading out of town, he saw a café that was open. Leaving Jana sleeping in the car, he rushed in, bought two double espressos, and some pastries, bread, cheese, and ham.

When he got back to the car, he found Jana awake and clutching a 9mm.

"You scared the crap out of me. Don't disappear like that."

"Sorry. Breakfast time. Did you get some decent sleep?"

They had switched driving duties three hours before and Jana had nodded off almost immediately

"I could use more, but I'll settle for this coffec. Thanks. Where are we?"

"Grosseto. We'll be at the marina in fifteen minutes."

"And then what? The marina will probably be closed at this hour."

"We'll find someone. Wake them up if we have to."

"We need to get scuba gear."

"I don't think we'll be able to rent any at this hour. Let's try to find the cave first. We don't have time to wait. Dr. Farag and his goons might be on the way."

They headed out. Jana opened up Dr. Farag's laptop and looked through his notes one last time.

“Remind me what he wrote about this place,” Jacob said. “I trawled through so many damn weird theories I can’t keep them straight.”

"Not much. He noted down, 'crypt in church not a natural cave.' He also noted 'caves mostly on the south part of the island.'"

“That helps.”

It did. the whole island was in the shape of a crescent, only a mile long.

“He also wrote ‘2019 storm erosion western shore. No caves uncovered.’”

“All right.”

“And then there’s this weird note. “Yorkshire. Mitchell never understood.”

“Yorkshire? As in the English county?”

“That’s what it says.”

“What’s that supposed to mean?”

“No idea. Apparently that ex-Marine didn’t either.”

"Are there any places named on the island called Yorkshire?"

“I checked. No. There are no English place names at all.”

“Huh. So I suggest we focus on the southern and southeastern parts of the island.”

“Sure, but how? We have no idea where this cave entrance is, assuming it even exists, and we don’t have any diving gear.”

“Why are you asking me? I’m just winging it.”

“There’s too much at stake to wing it.”

Jacob flashed her a grin. “Hey, it’s worked all the other times.”

Jana rolled her eyes and munched on her breakfast.

“That grin you think is so charming isn’t a guarantee of success,” she grumbled.

“It succeeded with you.”

“Har har. You’re forgiven, though. You found me breakfast.”

“And hopefully you can find me that cave.”

***

When they got off the boat they had hired from a sleepy-eyed sailor, toting some luggage filled with the terrorists’ weapons, Jana looked around at the little village clustered around the cove and decided she hadn’t seen a more peaceful place.

The village was barely a dozen houses, including a tourist shop/grocery store that was closed, and a café that was also closed. The soft sunlight of early morning bathed the stone walls in gold, and the cry of the seagulls was the only sound they heard other than the wind and waves.

Could an ancient atomic device really be hidden here along with a fortune in stolen gold and jewels?

This early, there were few people about, only a small fishing boat that had just docked after a night run. Three fishermen unloaded their catch.

“There’s a hotel just up that lane there,” their ride said, pointing to one of the two streets running from the port. “I don’t think it’s full, but if it is, there’s an Airbnb in the middle of the island. A nice cottage with good views. My sister runs it.”

“Thank you. We’ll check it out.”

"It's just at the foot of Monte Mario. You can find it on that map over there." The sailor pointed to a big map of the island printed on a signboard at the end of the pier.

“I’ll take a look,” Jana assured him. “Is there any place to rent scuba gear here on the island?”

“I’m afraid not. There’s a place on the mainland.”

Jana nodded. They had seen it by the port where they had hired this man. It wasn’t going to open for another two hours, and they had been in too much of a hurry.

They said goodbye to the sailor and walked up the pier.

Once out of earshot, Jacob spoke. “I suggest we walk to the southwest coast just where that storm hit and then search around the southern and eastern edges of the island where the sea caves are supposed to be.”

“Makes sense,” Jana said, stopping to look at the tourist map more to please the sailor than for any information.

Then her eyes settled on one detail, and her jaw dropped.

CHAPTER NINETEEN

Jana had that look again. Jacob knew it well. She got it anytime she had a eureka moment. He wished she'd shout out "Eureka!" That would be cute.

"What is it?" he asked her.

She pointed a shaky hand to a spot on the southern coast.

A cove marked "Cala Brigantina."

"Ummm, OK. You're going to have to help me out here."

"It means 'Bandit's cove' in Italian."

"So?"

"Brigantina is an Italian word, derived from Ancient Greek. The English word 'brigand' has the same derivation. It's also found in many other Indo-European languages. When the Emperor Claudius invaded Britain, he came across a tribe that was called the Brigantes."

"Wait. We were looking for British place names."

Jana nodded. "You know where the homeland of the Brigantes was? Yorkshire in northern England."

"Whoa. Dr. Farag must have known this. He must have thought this was an especially good candidate. That's why he wrote in code even on his own computer."

"That's what I'm thinking too."

"OK, but why did he think this was such a good place to look?"

"I don't know. That must have been in his other notes, the hard copies we never found."

"He probably still has them, or has memorized them enough that he might head straight here now that he's scratched off the top candidate on his list."

"We have to hurry." Jana took a photo of the map and they set out on the trail that would take them to Cala Brigantina.

***

Jacob didn't like the look of this at all. Cala Brigantina was a narrow cove barely fifty yards wide at its mouth and narrowing sharply to the end. Even though the weather was fair, waves pushed into the opening and crashed against the rear of the cove. There was no beach, only rugged limestone all the way down to the water's edge.

At least there were two factors in their favor—the water was relatively clear, a beautiful emerald green that would be photogenic if it didn't look so damn hazardous to swim in; and there was no one else around.

They picked their way down the rocks to the edge of the water, spray hitting them and making their footing on the rough rocks slick and unsteady. They found a relatively flat portion and paused.

"Did you bring a bathing suit?" Jacob asked.

"Or course not! Did you?"

"Nope. Let's go skinny dipping. I love skinny dipping."

"We'll wear our underwear," Jana grumbled, starting to strip down.

"You used to be fun." Jacob started stripping, too.

Once they were down to their underwear, Jacob savored the sight of the beautiful woman in front of him and then looked ruefully at the bag of weapons. "Pity we can't take these with us. I'd hate to find the cave and find either the Egyptians or the Libyans waiting for us."

"I thought modern small arms could withstand being submerged."

"They can, for a short time. But they'll get unreliable with prolonged exposure, especially if it's salt water. We'll need to be able to rely on these guns later. Besides, it makes it hard to swim. Didn't the story say that one of the German soldiers drowned?"

"Yeah. Apparently, the entrance is pretty long."

"Of course it is," Jacob grumbled. "Let's get to it."

"Maybe one of us should stand watch," Jana said scanning their surroundings.

"That will double the time it takes to find this place."

"All right. But let's try and make this quick."

They dove into the water and swam as deep as they could. The rhythmic movement of the waves tugged at them, but both were strong swimmers, and they were able to keep from getting tossed around too much.

By unspoken agreement, they split up to cover more of the area. Jacob searched to the west while Jana worked her way east. They would stay under the water as long as they could, working their arms and legs to maintain a position close to the rocks as the waves tugged them, searching every inch for any crevasse or opening.

It was slow, exhausting work. They could only search a few feet at a time before coming up for air, and when they went back under the surface, they wasted half their air finding the spot where they had left off.

Once, Jana found a hole that looked promising, but it turned out to only go back a few feet before ending. Jacob's portion was more eroded, and he had to peek and probe into many dark cracks, eliminating them one by one.

After a time, they took a break, lying on the flat rock where they had left the bag and clothes. Their breath came ragged, their eyes stung, and their muscles ached.

"We're not getting anywhere," Jana grumbled.

"It's going to take time. We'll find it."

Jana shook her head. "Assuming it's even here."

Jacob shrugged. "I'm not sure what else we can do."

Jana turned and looked up at the hilltop overlooking the cove.

"What?" Jacob asked.

"I thought I saw movement up there."

"Crap! Peeping Tom or something worse?"

"I don't know. I'm not sure I saw anything. Could have been a bird or something."

"Stay here. I'll go check."

Jacob unzipped the weapons bag, set a pistol behind a rock within each reach of Jana, and then toted the bag up the hill, still unzipped with an Uzi at the top ready for use.

He kept a sharp eye all around and tried to keep to cover as much as possible.

When he got to the top of the hill, he saw nothing. He made a quick survey of the nearest rocks big enough to hide a man and found no one. A pair of cyclists in the distance, heading to some other spot, made him retreat back down to the cove.

"False alarm," he told her once he got back. "But let's start searching again. No telling how long we're going to have this place to ourselves."

They dove back in, wasting their whole first breath and most of their second just trying to find to spots they had stopped at. Then began the slow, grueling search all over again.

Damn, there are so many little holes in this place, Jacob thought, probing yet another crevasse that turned out to be nothing. *We could be here all day.*

We'll take all day if we need to. We'll take all week.

But what if someone had found it already? This island was isolated but not uninhabited. He'd seen a few holiday homes scattered around the hills and fields on their way here. And the water was fairly clear. They couldn't have been the first people to look for sea caves, could they? Even if someone didn't know the legend of Rommel's treasure, they might just look for the hell of it.

And whoever came before would have been better equipped. They hadn't even had time to get some swimming goggles. His eyes were killing him. Maybe that little tourist shop by the pier would have some once it opened. It must be about nine by now.

But this was rural Italy. Nothing opened at nine. You counted yourself lucky if a place opened at all.

He broke the surface again, sputtering and wiping his eyes. They'd need a break again soon. Maybe he had the last of that food he'd bought back on the mainland.

A cry from Jana made him look. She was treading water about twenty yards away, waving one hand over her head.

"I think I found something!"

Jacob swam over to her.

"Right below me," she said, excited. "It's a hole, and I can't see or feel the end. And it's wide enough for both of us to go into. Remember how a pair of Germans was hauling an ammunition crate between them? This is big enough!"

"Let's go down and check it out. I'll go in while you stay at the entrance."

"Why?"

"Because it's too risky for both of us to go."

"I discovered it, so I should go."

"I'm the senior agent, so I get to make the call."

"Since when was I a CIA agent?" Jana asked, still treading water.

"Since you started sneaking along on these missions. You volunteered. And so, Ms. Volunteer, I'm going in first."

"Oh, all right. Let me show you."

They dove down, and Jana led him to a rough area of rock in which there were several dark holes and crevasses. She pointed to the deepest one, well out of sight from the surface, and Jacob swam into it.

Within a few strokes, he plunged into utter darkness. Jana was right, though, it was pretty big. He pointed his hands ahead of him and pumped with his legs, hoping to avoid bumping into a wall or something else, but that didn't stop him from bumping his head against a protrusion from the cave's ceiling.

The sharp, sudden pain stopped him short. After recovering for a moment, he swam forward again. Jacob's lungs began to burn. His right shoulder brushed against the side of the cave, and he shifted to the left, overcompensating and bumping into the left side. He bumped his head again and then a second time. It seemed the currents in this damn cave kept trying to pull him up.

Jacob began to struggle, his head pounding now. He needed some air. Fast.

And then the horrible realization hit.

He didn't have enough air to retrace his route and make it to the surface.

CHAPTER TWENTY

Jana treaded water, worry gnawing at her. Where the hell was Jacob? He should have surfaced by now. He must have run out of air by now, hadn't he?

Or maybe she wasn't accurately judging the time. It was hard to tell when she felt so nervous.

She decided to go down and check.

Pumping her arms and legs hard, she swam as fast as she could to the cave entrance. She hung on to the edge a moment, peering into the darkness.

Jacob was nowhere to be seen, not that she could really see anything in that inky hole.

Truly worried now, she swam into the cave.

And rammed right into Jacob, shooting out.

They spun around, limbs tangled with each other, until they both managed to get out of the cave and up to the surface, sputtering and coughing. Jana felt like she'd just swallowed half of the Tyrrhenian Sea.

"You OK?" she asked Jacob.

"Except for the big bump on my head. Actually four bumps. Three from the cave, and one from you."

"I thought you drowned."

"I nearly did. It takes almost your whole breath to make it through the tunnel. I came up into an empty space with air and found a shore made of small stones and sand. No light at all in there, but we've found our cave."

"Did you find anything? Were the crates there?"

"I didn't check. I came right back."

"What? How could you not check after all we've been through?"

He grinned. "Because I wanted you to make the discovery."

Jana's heart melted. "Really? You did that for me?"

"My winning smile is winning this time, isn't it?"

She kissed him. "Yes."

"I thought so. We should go in together. It's too dangerous to make the trip alone. Let's see what's there."

See? Jana wished they could. They didn't have any source of light. The best they could hope for is to crawl around and try to find the ammunition boxes by feel. If they found something, they'd have to return better prepared.

"Ready?" Jacob asked. "The tunnel is pretty much straight. Careful with the ceiling."

"All right."

They took a series of deep breaths, then dove in. Jacob let Jana take the lead.

Darkness enveloped her. She trusted Jacob's word and kept swimming, angling down slightly to keep from hitting the tunnel ceiling.

She hit it anyway, scraping it with her shoulders. Angling down a bit more, she kept going, scraped the left side of the tunnel, and briefly got tangled with Jacob when she slowed down too much.

Jana continued on as the air in her lungs grew stale and her body burned for oxygen. Her teeth gritted, her limbs began to feel rubbery, and still she moved forward.

And then, a subtle change in the water. It felt like it was moving around in more directions than simply back and forth, and the temperature had cooled half a degree or so. It felt, and Jana couldn't explain why she sensed this, that there was more of it somehow.

She angled up, arms stretched before her, and didn't hit a stony ceiling.

Instead, she broke the surface and gulped air.

Jana treaded water for a moment, gasping as her lungs heaved, filling with sweet, sweet oxygen. Her breaths echoed back to her like a hundred gasping ghosts.

Jacob broke the surface close by, but she couldn't see a thing.

"I made it!" she cried out.

Made it ... made it ... made it ...

"Great! Swim forward."

Forward ... forward ... forward ...

She did, and in a few feet, hit against a beach of sand and pebbles, scraping her hands and knees.

Jana didn't care. They had found the cave! Could Rommel's treasure really be here?

"You make it?" Jana asked. She couldn't see a thing.

"Yeah," Jacob replied from closer than she had anticipated.

She reached out and touched him. They felt around until they clasped hands.

“Go on,” Jacob urged. “Go find what you’re looking for.”

She got on her hands and knees and tugged his hand. “Come with me.”

“OK, but a little behind. This discovery is yours.”

She crawled forward, groping ahead of her.

And then her hand touched something cold and hard and flat.

Metal. A vertical surface of metal.

She moved her hand along the flat surface and came to a corner. Moving her hand up, she came to a flat top. Heart beating fast, she swept her hand along the top and found a metal handle.

Jana let out a little laugh of joy, moving both hands all over the object. Yes, it was rectangular. Yes, there were handles on each side. Yes, there was a seam at the top.

She could feel the corrosion all over the metal. It had been sitting here in this cave full of damp, salty air for eighty years. But it was intact.

And it had all the dimensions of an ammunition crate.

"I found it!" she said, her words stumbling out with her laughter. "I really found it."

She felt Jacob move up beside her, their hands roving over the old German crate together.

“There should be more,” Jana said. “Let’s find them.”

They moved around the crate, splitting up. Almost immediately, Jacob said. "I found another one!"

“Same dimensions as the last one?”

“Yeah. Let’s find that double crate that Italian source mentioned. That should have the Staff of Ra in it.”

They continued their blind crawl around the cave. Jana found two more ammunition crates, and Jacob another, before Jana worked her way back deeper into the cave, away from the water, and came across another crate. Running her hands along it, she discovered it was longer than the others.

About twice as long. As if two ammunition crates had been attached end to end.

Just as the Italian officer had said.

So why had he gotten the location wrong? Had he deliberately lied in his own diary, or had the crates been moved by someone else?

Or maybe his shipment had been only one of two, and the double crate held a duplicate staff.

The staff that circulated on the black market and ended up in Dawson's hands.

The realization hit her like a tidal wave. If that were so, then she had her hands on the crate that contained …

"The Staff of Ra. The real one. I've found it."

Jacob moved toward her, following the sound of her voice. Again, they felt around the crate together.

"Let's find the catch to open it," Jacob said. "There should be catches along the top."

Jana found one and tried to flip it open. It wouldn't budge. From Jacob's grunts, she could tell he struggled with one too.

"They're too corroded, Jacob, but we've got it. Let's get out of here and come back better equipped."

"Sounds like a plan, we—"

Jacob's words cut off as light suddenly shone in the cave.

CHAPTER TWENTY ONE

Jacob blinked and looked over his shoulder. A light shone beneath the water in the little underground lake that took up about a third of the cave. He could see the rest of the cave, about the size of two large living rooms, completely enclosed by a low ceiling about eight feet high and rough limestone walls. He saw no other way out.

The light grew brighter and broke the surface.

A shadowy figure rose with it. Two more lights appeared in the water to either side of the figure.

One of the flashlight beams caught the figure at the front.

Hamza.

Dr. Farag's righthand man and the other two terrorists.

They all wore bathing suits and pulled long knives from sheaths strapped to their waists.

"Dr. Farag says thank you for finding this place," Hamza said.

"You've been following us all this time?" Jacob asked, backing away. His eyes darted to and fro, looking for a weapon, any weapon to hold off these three trained fighters.

"Yes. He salutes you for being smarter than he is."

"Didn't have the strength to swim in here himself, eh?"

Hamza chuckled. "The doctor is a great warrior for jihad, but in his own way. He is not a fighter like us. Now you will die like fighters, and we will take the Staff of Ra. The Eternal City with be an eternal ruin and that will start a war that will end in Sharia law over the whole world!"

Jacob reached down, grabbed the biggest rock he could find, and whipped it at Hamza.

The terrorist moved remarkably fast for someone so big, and ducked it. The stone intended for his head flew close over him and smacked into the face of the man behind, who let out a grunt and fell back into the water with a splash.

With a roar, Hamza and the other terrorist launched themselves out of the water and charged.

Hamza came at Jacob, while the other man went for Jana.

They had no time to grab more rocks.

Hamza pulled himself up short, just out of reach of Jacob, and then came in slowly, leading with his knife and shining his flashlight at Jacob's face to blind him. Jacob kept his eyes fixed on the man's feet, trying to anticipate the inevitable thrust or slash from how he stepped.

There it was, a sudden feint to the left, then a dart right and forward. Jacob backed off, the knife's keen edge missing him by an inch.

They began to circle each other, Jacob keeping his arms wide, waiting for a chance for a grapple. From the sounds of movement not far off, Jana was in a similar situation. He had to get to her, had to help her. While surprisingly good in a fight, she didn't have his level of hand-to-hand training.

Or Hamza's. His next thrust nearly gutted him. Jacob had to jerk to the right to avoid it, only to strike one of the ammunition crates and stumble.

Hamza was on him in a heartbeat. Jacob dodged again, felt a hot pain along his right forearm, then grabbed the man's knife hand with his left.

Hamza struggled and kicked, then lashed out with his flashlight.

The blow caught Jacob in the side of the head, making his knees buckle. Hamza struggled to pull his knife hand from Jacob's vice grip, failed, and raised his flashlight again.

Jacob slammed his right fist into Hamza's groin. A shock of pain went up his own injured arm, but what Hamza experienced must have felt ten times worse. The terrorist roared in agony, doubling over.

But he did not let go of the knife.

Jacob took care of that by grabbing the knife hand with both of his own and twisting it back. He endured a weak blow to his shoulders from the flashlight, then managed to force Hamza to drop the knife.

Another glancing blow to the head by that damn flashlight, which miraculously still shone. Waterproof, too. The Sword of the Righteous came prepared. Must have all been Boy Scouts.

Jacob gut punched him, then followed with an uppercut. While his own strikes were weakened by the abuse he'd taken, it was still enough for Hamza to fall hard on his back.

Jacob grabbed the knife and whirled around, just in time to see Jana on the floor about ten feet away, the other terrorist straddling her. He was pressing down with his knife, Jana gripping his arm with both hands, the knife inching relentlessly down toward her eye.

He rushed for them. There was a splashing in the water, but Jacob didn't have time to look if reinforcements were arriving.

Jacob came in low and fast, planting Hamza's knife neatly between the terrorist's ribs. The man let out a grunt. Jacob withdrew the knife and kicked him off Jana.

A shout from the water made him turn.

The man he had beamed with the rock had gotten back up, face streaming with blood. He carried a waterproof rubber bag that he had unzipped. He pulled an UZI from it and tossed the weapon to Hamza, who was just getting to his feet.

"Into the water!" Jacob shouted.

He dove straight under. His last sight was the terrorist pulling out another gun from the waterproof bag.

Jacob swam right for him, the terrorist's legs and waist a wavering vision in the churning water.

He wrapped his arms around the man, ignoring the sting of his knife wound in the salt water, planted his feet on the cave floor, and hauled him up.

Jacob ended up flipping the terrorist and pushing him face-first into the water.

A bang of metal against his forearm. The gun. Jacob grabbed it, twisted, and felt a rush of water as the guy pulled the trigger. He prayed those bullets wouldn't hit Jana. They couldn't go too far underwater, but still.

Jacob struggled with the terrorist for possession of the gun. His opponent landed a painful kick to his kneecap, and Jacob let go. The terrorist fumbled the gun, and it sank to the bottom.

Jacob came up for air, slugged the terrorist for good measure, and looked around. Jana treaded water nearby.

"Look out!" she shouted.

Jacob went back underwater. He pushed Jana toward the tunnel as bullets pushed through the water around them, leaving eerie white streaks in their wake.

Jana took the hint and swam fast for the tunnel. Jacob hoped she had enough air in her lungs to make the trip back out to the cove. He wasn't sure he did.

The light didn't penetrate far into the tunnel, and pretty soon they were swimming in darkness again. Jacob's forearm stung, but his lungs stung more. No, he hadn't gotten enough air in his lungs. The last two times he had gone through here, he had taken several deep breaths and dove in fully prepared. He hadn't had time to do that now.

He kept pumping his arms and legs. Jacob ended up moving too fast and getting kicked in the wounded arm by Jana.

That messed up his stroke, and by the time he got it together again, bumped into the ceiling, and got back on course, his lungs felt like they were on fire.

But he had no choice but to keep moving. Hamza and the other terrorist might be closing in on them. They couldn't go back, couldn't pause, and might not be able to make it by going forward.

He felt his limbs growing weaker, his thoughts becoming muddled. It took all his willpower to keep moving and to keep his lungs from inhaling.

Suddenly, the darkness was replaced by dim light. He could just make out Jana swimming in front of him. Then she was up and out of sight.

Up. The urge shot through his foggy mind like an SOS signal. He shot upwards at an angle, clipped the cave mouth with his feet, and pumped with the last of his strength up toward the sun-dappled surface.

He broke through to air and took the biggest gulp of that sweet gas in his life.

Jacob treaded water, gulping in air, until the sound of gunfire woke him up.

Dr. Moswen Farag stood on the rocks about twenty yards away, firing an UZI at them.

CHAPTER TWENTY TWO

Much as Jana would have liked nothing better than to drag herself onto the rocks and sleep for ten hours, bullets plonking into the water all around her galvanized her into action. She took a deep breath and went below the surface again.

Jacob swam past her, headed for the mouth of the cove. Jana followed.

After about ten yards, she broke the surface to get a breath and immediately went back under. She swam as far as she could and repeated the motion.

On the third time up, she wiped her eyes and dared a look behind her. Jacob came up a moment later.

Dr. Farag was running along the shoreline, trying to fit a new magazine into the UZI. Just as he did so, he slipped and landed on his rear end.

Jacob laughed, cupped his hands, and shouted, “Amateur!”

They were too far away to rush him before he got himself together, so they kept swimming toward the mouth of the cove.

The waves tried to push them back, and Jana’s weary limbs struggled to keep her moving forward. No way she was going to stay here, though. She had no idea what they’d do next. First, survival.

They got close to the opening of the cove and angled left to make it to the rocks just on the inside of the curve of the cove's mouth. There they clung to the slick stones, panting and weary. They could see Dr. Farag standing guard about halfway between the cave and them, out of range. Beyond him, they could clearly see their clothes and the weapons bag still lying where they'd left them.

Another bag sat beside it, obviously the terrorists’. Jana wondered what was in it.

Then Hamza broke the surface close to the cave. As soon as he did, he seemed to sink back into the water. He struggled for a moment before the other terrorist appeared. The pair swam in tandem for the nearest stretch of shoreline, shouting something Jana couldn’t catch.

Dr. Farag picked his way along the rocks toward them, stopping every few yards to turn back and check on Jana and Jacob.

Hamza and the other terrorist struggled out of the water, hauling an ammunition crate between them.

One that was twice as long as the others.

Jana watched, helpless, as they set the crate down. Hamza struggled to his feet and tried to open the corroded latches while his companion slumped on the rocks, obviously worn out.

"What do we do?" Jana said, lying against the rock and trying to rest.

"We should get out of here," Jacob replied through gasps for air. "Warn people."

"Warn who? There's no real town here. No police."

"We have to get to the port before they do. Try to get a boat to the mainland."

Dr. Farag made it to the others and pulled out something from a bag he had brought with him.

Jana squinted and saw it was a Geiger counter.

He leaned over the crate, passing the Geiger counter over it. Then he leapt back. Dr. Farag gestured to his two men, who started to get dressed. Dr. Farag picked up Jacob and Jana's clothes and weapons bag and looked like he planned to take them with him.

"Let's go," Jana said. "We've seen enough."

Enough to know he's got the real thing. I wonder how much radiation it's leaking.

They dove back in the water and swam out of the cove. The short rest and the knowledge that The Sword of the Righteous had finally gotten its hand on the Libyan Staff of Ra galvanized them into renewed efforts. They broke through the waves rushing into the cove and swam out for a bit before cutting east toward the shoreline that would eventually take them back to the little port that was the island's only contact with the outside world.

Once they got on land, they forced themselves up the rocky slope to the grassy, hilly plain that took up much of the island's interior.

They were soon greeted by a terrible sight.

An old pickup truck drove away from the cave site, Hamza and the crate in back. It was already quarter of a mile away and its occupants didn't seem to see them.

"They stole a truck," Jana said. *And probably killed whoever they stole it from.*

Her suspicions got terribly confirmed as the truck passed the two bicyclists Jacob had seen before. As they came alongside the unsuspecting young man and woman, Hamza sprayed them with UZI fire. They tumbled to the side of the road and lay still.

"No!" Jacob cried.

They began to run across the plain, soaking wet and still dressed only in their underwear. There was no chance of catching up with them, nothing they could do even if they did, but they ran anyway. The truck dwindled into the distance, the faint crackle of gunfire coming back to them as if in mockery, and then the truck drove out of sight.

***

Evening was already falling when Tyler Wallace walked into the police station at Grosseto to pick up his wayward agent.

The day before, he had been alerted to the danger Jacob and Jana were in. A ghost had told him.

Because that's sure what it felt like when he picked up his secured line and Aaron Peters gave the right code words.

Not that Tyler needed them. He'd know that man's voice anywhere.

And when that ghost told him a trio of assassins were tailing Jacob and Jana in Taranto, he knew he needed to get on it. No matter that he still felt weak and his arm was in a sling. He had work to do.

Because just that morning, there'd been a terror attack at Pescara, a port on Italy's eastern coast not far from Rome.

Tyler Wallace kept tabs on any terror activity in the Mediterranean region, and this had been an unusual one. A private yacht registered in Greece had docked in Pescara. The harbormaster thought it suspicious that all the men on board were young, well-built Arabs and decided to search the boat.

He must have found something because they attacked him.

The harbormaster and the police officer who had come along with him managed to shout out a warning and radio for backup before they were killed.

The Arabs on board the yacht then panicked, shooting up the marina and killing several innocent civilians before stealing a delivery van and speeding away. Witnesses said they had loaded a large crate and several heavy-looking bags into the back of the van before leaving.

The last reports indicated the police had found the delivery van ditched by the side of the highway several miles down the road. The assumption was that they had secured another vehicle.

Tyler Wallace had been in this business too long to believe in coincidences, so he had taken the first flight to Rome.

When he had heard that there had been another attack on the isolated island of Giannutri and that two Americans had been detained on suspicion of being involved, he knew where he needed to go.

And so now, flanked by a member of the Italian secret service and an officer in the Carabinieri, Italy's national police force, he walked into the little police station in the town of Grosseto and demanded to see his agents.

The desk sergeant looked at the secret service man's ID, then at the Carabinieri, and went pale.

"You mean they were telling the truth?" he asked in English.

"What do you mean?" Wallace demanded.

"They were saying some crazy story about some Egyptians stealing an ancient artifact from a sea cave. The guy said he was CIA but didn't have any ID. He didn't even have any clothes."

"Jesus! Take us to them right now!"

The abashed local cop took them into the lockup, where Wallace found Jacob and Jana sitting glumly in adjoining cells wearing prison jumpsuits. Jacob had a bandage around his right forearm.

Jacob's look of surprise when Wallace walked into the holding area made it all almost worth it. Usually, Agent Snow surprised him, not the other way around, and never in a good way.

"Let them out," he told the police officer.

"But—"

A snapped order in Italian by the Carabinieri got the local cop moving. Wallace turned to Jacob.

"So they have it?"

Jacob nodded. "They have it."

"Any idea where they might have gone?"

Jacob shrugged and hung his head. "I failed, sir. They surprised us and chased us off. Then they went on a rampage on the island. The cops say they killed eight people and wounded fifteen more. Just shot down anyone they came across."

Jacob's voice broke at this last sentence.

"That's on them, Agent Snow," Wallace said in a soft voice.

Jacob didn't look at him. This was one of Agent Snow's few weak points—he always took any collateral damage personally. A good sign for a human being, a major liability for a CIA agent.

"Rome."

Jana’s voice made them turn. She was just stepping out of her cell after the policeman released her.

“Why do you say that A- … Ms. Peters?” He had almost referred to her as “Agent Peters.”

“Something one of the terrorists said. He said the Eternal City would be an eternal ruin. Rome’s nickname is the Eternal City.”

“It’s even worse than we thought,” the Italian secret agent said.

Wallace had told him that Jacob and Jana were trying to track down The Sword of the Righteous, made famous for their attack on the Suez Canal, and that they may very well be trying to construct a nuclear device. The yacht crew that had shot its way through Pescara must have been carrying that device. All they needed was the uranium, and it looked like Dr. Farag had secured it.

They all walked out of the station.

“We’ll get you some civilian clothes and gear,” Wallace told them. “Any idea where in the city they might hit?”

“If the device is big enough, they can set it off anywhere in the city,” Jacob said.

Wallace shivered. Rome made the perfect target. Pescara was only a two-hour drive from Rome. Grosseto was slightly less.

Dr. Farag and his bomb crew could have easily met up by now. They were no doubt assembling the bomb at that very moment.

A bomb they would use to destroy a European capital. Not only that, but one of the great symbols of Western civilization and also the seat of the Vatican, the holiest spot for one of Christianity’s biggest faiths.

A war between East and West, Muslim and Christian, would be inevitable.

And it would consume the world for decades.

CHAPTER TWENTY THREE

Jacob felt miserable. He had been helpless to stop the slaughter on the island. If only he had prepared better for the dive. If only he had trusted the CIA to ask for backup, someone to guard the surface while he and Jana had gone down. If only … if only …

The logical part of his mind knew none of this was his fault. They were chasing around at a frantic pace, unable to trust even his own organization after what Aaron Peters had told him. There was nothing else he could have done.

But the larger part of his mind, the one filled with duty, berated himself for not stopping Dr. Farag and his goons.

And this second attack at Pescara … that had been the delivery. It made sense. Dr. Farag knew he was hunted, and couldn't risk moving the Staff of Ra too far. It would be better for the bomb makers to come to him so they could destroy the nearest major city.

The terrorists would be assembling the bomb right now if they hadn't finished assembling it already.

He thought of all this as he sped down the highway on a motorcycle, Jana clinging behind him. Wallace had gotten them clothing, phones, this bike, and a pair of pistols.

"Sorry, I can't get you more," he had told them. "I'll gear you up better once we're in Rome."

With that, Jacob and Jana had sped off. Wallace was following in a police car, in radio and satellite phone conversation with every intelligence agency in Europe.

Rome had been warned. Even though it was now fully night, the police, the Carabinieri, the secret service, and the army had all been mobilized. Their combined forces were rounding up everyone on the terror watch list, checking every truck, and guarding every public place.

Jacob knew it wouldn't do any good. Dr. Farag was too smart to fall afoul of a simple dragnet.

No, he would have planned ahead. Established a safehouse. The Sword of the Righteous had enough reach that there had probably been a safehouse prepared in every European capital for years.

This was common practice for lots of terror groups. The safehouse would be owned by some innocuous Muslim who ran a little shop and kept his nose clean. Someone who didn’t go to radical mosques and whose Internet search history was above suspicion. They might even get ballsy and join an interfaith coalition, calling for better understanding between the world’s religions.

But secretly, he would be a one-man sleeper cell, staying quiet until activated.

That innocuous man with the little shop would be hosting them now, smiling at his neighbors and maintaining the façade as Dr. Farag and his team assembled a nuclear device in his spare room.

But where? Where?

He had no idea.

Rome was a city of three million people. They could be anywhere.

They came to the first of the roadblocks twenty miles outside town. Cars and trucks were backed up half a mile deep, except for one lane the cops kept open for emergency traffic. Jacob slowed as he approached the cop directing traffic. The man took one look at his police pass and waved him through.

Good, all the roadblocks had been warned of their arrival, just as Wallace had promised. They could get into town in no time.

And then what? Go knocking door to door, asking who's got the bomb?

“Got any ideas about the location?” Jacob shouted over his shoulder.

“How big of an explosion would it be?”

“Big enough to level the whole city center. Bad radiation for the rest of the city.”

“He’d want to set it off close to the Vatican, level St. Peters and all the other buildings and make sure the Pope and everyonc else there was dead. So he’d place it somewhere near the city center.”

“That leaves way too much ground to cover. Can’t you narrow it down?”

Jana was quiet for a moment. "We might want to try the Egyptian Institute. It's a cultural building set up by the Egyptian government years ago. A small Egyptian community has grown up around it. When I was doing background research on Dr. Farag, I noticed he had given a bunch of talks there over the years."

“Is it close to the center of town?”

“Close enough. It’s only about a mile from the Vatican as the crow flies.”

“Yeah, close enough. Direct us there. We might be too late already.”

Jacob kept speeding along, passing the line of idling vehicles and approaching the roadblock he could see just ahead. They’d let him pass just as quickly as that traffic cop had.

Suddenly, a car pulled out of the line and got right in front of them.

Jacob hit the brakes and swerved.

Not quick enough. They hit the car and Jacob went end over end over the hood to land hard on the pavement beyond. His head cracked against the road and even protected by a helmet the impact was enough to shake him.

He lay there for a second, too stunned to move.

Jacob turned his head to look at the car that had blocked their path, his neck twinging painfully.

He saw two well-built Anglo men rush out of the car, grab Jana from where she lay on the ground, and bundle her into the back.

Jacob staggered to his feet, fumbling for his gun as the nearby motorists stared.

“Go get Dr. Farag!” Jana shouted through the open back window of the car. “Forget about me! It won’t matter if you don’t stop him!”

Jacob walked like a drunk man toward the car, finally managing to draw his gun and nearly dropping it in the process.

A gun poked out of the back seat of the car, the gunman reaching across Jana. She batted the gun aside, and the shot went wide. The car made a 180 and started moving away.

“Get Dr. Farag!” Jana shouted.

Jacob was tempted to fire at the vehicle’s tires, but there were cars and pedestrians all over. Many of the drivers had jumped out of their vehicles at the sound of the shot and were running in all directions. He couldn’t risk hitting one.

A police car, sirens wailing, shot past him after the vehicle. Jacob bit his lip. He knew it would do no good.

That had been The Order. He was sure of it. This wasn’t the first time they’d kidnapped Jana.

Hobbling over to his motorcycle, he found one of the wheels had been twisted by the impact.

“Damn it!”

He couldn’t pursue. Even worse, he shouldn’t pursue.

Because Jana was right. If Dr. Farag set off the bomb, nothing would matter anymore. He'd die, Jana would die, the kidnappers would die.

And three million more people would die.

Jacob groaned, feeling as helpless as he had been witnessing the slaughter on the island. But he had to go. He had to check out that neighborhood that Jana had told him about.

The last thing she had ever gotten to tell him?

Focus. This mission wasn't about his feelings. It wasn't even about his life, or Jana's. It had grown far, far bigger than that.

But to simply leave her …

… and for what? A hunch about a neighborhood that Dr. Farag used to hang out in during his previous life? That was the slimmest of all possible leads. It barely counted as a lead at all.

And yet it was the only lead anyone had.

With a supreme force of will, Jacob Snow turned around and limped to the roadblock up ahead, ready to use the carte blanche the Italian police had given him to its fullest extent.

If he didn't manage to stop the bomb, getting incinerated with the rest of the city would come as a relief, because he could never live with himself for letting the CIA down, for letting Rome down, for letting the whole world down.

And most of all, for letting Jana down.

CHAPTER TWENTY FOUR

Jana sat in the back seat of the car, pressed between two burly men, each with a pistol dug into her ribs.

Here we go again. This is just like Mexico.

She knew from bitter experience that reasoning with them didn't make any difference. Pleading would get her nowhere. And threats? These people were willing to chew on cyanide to avoid capture.

But maybe she could bait them. Knock them off balance. It would be unpredictable for a captive to do that, and maybe that would trip them up.

She had nothing to lose. This whole place could get nuked any second, and they were obviously under orders not to kill her.

Although her heart was racing, she forced her muscles to relax. Then she cleared her throat and, in as calm a voice as possible, said,

"You guys are with The Order, aren't you?"

They didn't respond.

"I mean, I can tell by the way you guys roll. Must be pretty mad that my father has been taking you out one by one."

They remained silent.

"If you're going to take me anywhere, I suggest out of the city."

"You know what this fuss is about?" the driver asked, looking at her in the rearview mirror. He was Italian. The two guys flanking her were Anglo.

"Don't you know?" She waited for a reply, and when she didn't get one, decided to be honest. "The Sword of the Righteous is planning on setting off a nuclear device in the city center of Rome."

The driver let out a curse in Italian.

"Keep your eye on the road!" one of the gunmen in back shouted.

They were speeding down the highway, and the flashing lights of a police car could be seen about a hundred yards behind them, closing fast.

"Looks like you're not as efficient as the other teams we've met," Jana said. "I guess my dad killed all your top operatives, huh?"

The gunman who had spoken jammed the muzzle of his pistol hard into Jana's side.

"Shut up!"

The police car began to close. One of the gunmen leaned out the window and fired three quick shots, causing the police car to swerve and slow to a stop, steam billowing from under the hood. Jana wanted to push the shooter out the window but didn't dare try anything with the other man's pistol jammed against her midriff.

Once they had shaken the police car, the driver took them onto an exit a few miles away from the roadblock and drove to a small residential area. They parked right behind a van. The van's back opened up and another Italian motioned impatiently for them get inside.

"You're taking me in a van?" Jana said with contempt. "Don't you know that every cop and soldier in Italy is checking every van they see? Maybe they'll think you have the nuke, just get trigger happy, and just shoot first and ask questions later."

Another jab with the gun. "You think you're going to distract us by all this? Shut up and get out of the car!"

I think I'm already distracting you. Maybe enough that I'll get a chance to try something.

She stepped out, keeping a wary eye on her abductors.

"What's this about a nuclear device?" the other gunman asked.

"That's what Jacob and I were tracking when you cut in and ruined our plans. You idiots, you're going to have a lot of blood on your hands."

That didn't seem to faze them in the least. They bundled her into the back of the van and closed the door.

"Where is this bomb?" the Italian driver asked.

"We don't know exactly. Somewhere in the city center. It could go off any minute. How about you help stop it?"

"None of our business," the driver said, putting her hands behind her and securing them with zip cuffs. Her shoulder throbbed with pain. She'd landed hard on her right side, and it felt like that entire half of her body was swelling into one big bruise. "Thank you for the warning, though. We'll get away from the city as fast as possible. They'll only be checking vans going toward Rome, not away from it."

Jana looked into his eyes. "You're Italian. You want to see Rome get nuked? You want to see three million of your countrymen killed or suffer radiation burns? You want the best of your nation's heritage destroyed?"

The look of complete unconcern that he gave her shocked her to her core.

"I'm not Italian. We are beyond nationhood."

They sat her down in the back of the van. The two Italians got into the front while the others stayed to guard her.

As the van pulled away, Jana struggled not to give way to despair.

The Order was even worse than she expected. While they hadn't been behind this attack, or at least not to the knowledge of these grunts, they looked at it with utter indifference.

She could already hear one of the guys in front talking on a cell phone, keeping his voice down so she couldn't make out his words. No doubt he was talking to his commander, relaying what Jana had told him. The high command would then discuss it, weighing the pros and cons.

Maybe they'd join the hunt for the bombers. Maybe they'd sit by and do nothing. She had no idea, because she had no idea what The Order actually wanted.

What she did know was that if those in charge of this shadowy organization decided that Rome getting leveled would further their agenda, they'd stand by and let it happen.

And if it neither hurt nor helped their agenda, they'd stand by too.

This organization, whatever they wanted, was deeply evil. At least Dr. Farag and his slimy crew came out and said what their goals were. At least they took responsibility for their actions and didn't hide in the shadows more than they needed to survive.

The Order would do whatever, and by any means, to attain their goals.

The van sped down a dark suburban road that had no streetlights, only occasionally passing housing developments. Few cars were out. The radio and TV had been calling out warnings of an impending terror attack for a couple of hours now. The Italian government hadn't revealed that it was a nuke, only mentioning the threat of a "major strike" against the capital. Wise decision. Word of a nuke would cause such a panic that security forces wouldn't be able to move.

No one thought to blindfold her like last time, and that made Jana wonder. Were they simply rattled by the revelation that they faced annihilation, or didn't they care that she saw where they were going?

Did they plan to kill her?

No. At least not yet. They could have killed her as she lay stunned on the pavement.

Her whole right side, the side on which she landed, ached. Nothing seemed broken, although her right shoulder and neck felt the worst. It sure didn't help having her hands tied behind her. She still wore her helmet, and her head throbbed inside it as if the helmet was two sizes too small.

The van slowed to a stop on a darkened stretch of the road. One of the gunmen opened the back.

"Get out."

Jana stepped out. A dark field stretched to one side. On the other was a gas station, closed due to the emergency.

She saw an SUV with tinted windows parked ahead of them. Another vehicle change. She heard a helicopter in the distance but didn't see the lights.

They had obviously planned this carefully, right down to being in that waiting line of vehicles just when she and Jacob came up.

There was a mole in the CIA. It was the only explanation. And it had to be someone really high up.

They approached the SUV. No one moved inside.

"Come on!" one of the gunmen at her side said. "We got to keep moving."

The back of the SUV slid open, and a hand appeared.

A hand chucking a grenade.

A chorus of shouts as everyone threw themselves down. Jana bolted for the open field, ducking low, hoping the shrapnel didn't tear her apart, half wishing it would to deny The Order any leverage with Jacob and her father.

A loud bang and a flash, and Jana found herself flying through the air.

She landed in the field, hitting the soil face first, unable to break her fall with her shackled wrists.

Jana lay there, half unconscious, ears ringing.

A stun grenade.

The surprising realization came through the haze. The grenade hadn't been intended to kill. Who had thrown it?

Better not stick around and find out. Jana tried to struggle to her feet but only landed on her face again. The sharp pain of that woke her up a bit, enough to feel the hot blood pouring out of her nose. Broken? Probably.

She rolled onto her side and struggled up to her knees. Looking over her shoulder, she saw a dark figure walking away from the road. All her captors lay sprawled and unmoving. Had he killed them all?

And now he was coming for her.

Jana managed to raise herself on wobbly legs and start staggering away. Although she could hear nothing over the ringing in her ears, she knew the man was after her. Or he might just shoot her in the back.

She ran in a zigzag, tense and waiting for the bullet that was sure to come.

Instead, she felt a firm yet gentle hand grab her shoulder and turn her around.

She staggered, stumbled, and then righted herself.

And found she was facing her father.

CHAPTER TWENTY FIVE

"How is the situation outside?" Dr. Farag asked.

"Chaotic," the kebab shop owner told him. "The police are rounding up people left and right."

They sat in the living room of the shop owner's house, a large four-bedroom place that he could have never afforded without the deep pockets of The Sword of the Righteous. The shop owner, whose name was Ibrahim, acted as a host to any jihadists passing through Rome. He was above suspicion, and had already prepared for his martyrdom.

"Rounding up our people?" Dr. Farag asked.

"They've raided every righteous mosque in the city. They've brought in hundreds of Muslims."

"Is the community protesting?"

"Not that I've seen. Every Muslim is laying low. I didn't stay out for long. Too risky. There are no Muslims on the streets right now. There's hardly anyone on the streets except police and army."

Dr. Farag scratched his chin. While Ibrahim had a spotless criminal record and had avoided open ties with known Islamists, this was an Egyptian neighborhood. The police were bound to start house-to-house searches sooner or later.

He had acted hasty in coming to this obvious place. Someone might track him here. But what choice did he have? With those CIA agents after him, there hadn't been time to get the Staff of Ra out of the country. It had been safer and quicker to have the crew with the prepared bomb come to them.

Rome had been near the top of his hit list anyway—the pride of Western civilization, the seat of the Catholic church, and the capital of one of Europe's biggest economies. Thousands of tourists from around the world. There had been many good reasons to hit Rome.

And they would. The bomb crew was almost ready now.

The three engineers were in one of the rooms, wearing Tyvek suits and fitting the uranium into the detonation device. They had lined the room with lead sheeting as much as they could, but everyone knew radiation was leaking out. Dr. Farag could practically feel it slicing through his DNA and wreaking havoc on his cell structure.

The thought made him shiver. What a horrible way to die!

"You all right, Doctor?"

Dr. Farag blinked. He had forgotten Ibrahim was there.

"Yes, just excited."

Ibrahim grinned. "Only another hour or so, yes?"

"Maybe less. It's time I got prepared."

"There are razors in the bathroom," the kebab shop owner told him. "I stocked up for this day."

Dr. Farag nodded and walked upstairs, trembling a bit as he did so. The technicians were in one of the upstairs bedrooms, and every step brought him closer to that horrible invisible sun that was burning his insides.

It doesn't matter, he tried to convince himself. *Soon you will be in Paradise and your body will be as pure as the young maidens who will live in your heavenly garden.*

At the top of the stairs he gave a fearful look at the sealed door, then went down the hall in the other direction, passing a bedroom where a couple of the jihadists were praying, and past another darkened room where Hamza stood guard, peeking out of a tiny slit in the Venetian blinds at the street.

"Any movement?" Dr. Farag whispered.

"A police car passed by ten minutes ago. It didn't slow down. Nothing since."

"God is protecting us."

I hope He will protect me against the radiation.

It doesn't matter. You will be in Paradise long before you develop cancer, he told himself for the hundredth time that day.

His mother had died of cancer in Cairo's ramshackle central hospital in a noisy room with five other female patients. His family didn't have money for chemotherapy, and the drugs they could buy for her did little other than to ease a bit of her pain.

Only a bit. She had died moaning, calling out to Allah, in terrible torment.

He did not want to die the same death. Better to go out in a painless flash, to become a martyr for the future of the true faith.

Dr. Farag continued to the bathroom, where he said a quick prayer and then stripped naked. He grabbed a razor and some shaving cream and began to shave his leg hair. Once that was done, he turned his attention to his armpits, chest, and eventually his pubic hair.

In a few minutes, he had no hair left except what was on his head. A suicide bomber must be clean of all body hair to be pure enough to commit the act. He would not get a proper burial. There would be nobody to wash and anoint, so they had all gone through this ritual as compensation.

Dr. Farag looked at himself in the mirror, as hairless as he had been as an innocent child. He smiled at himself. Yes, he was pure, and he was willing.

He checked his watch. Within a few minutes, half an hour at most, the bomb would be ready, and he himself would push the button that would detonate it and bring on World War Three.

***

Now, what the hell do I do?

Jacob stood in the doorway of a shuttered kebab shop, studying the Egyptian Institute across the street. It was a large stone building in a modern style with a couple of ancient sculptures of pharaohs in the front garden. No lights shone inside, and the gate was locked.

He noted a lot of the shop signs, while in Italian, had the Halal symbol or referred to various countries in the Middle East. He was in the right neighborhood, the one Jana had told him about, but he had no idea what to do now.

It had taken him ages to get here, having to stop and show his ID at a dozen different roadblocks. While they had all waved him through, it took time, time he knew he couldn't afford.

All these closed shops, all these houses with the blinds drawn. How was he to know which one, if any, was the terrorists' safehouse?

At every roadblock, he had asked for a Geiger counter, wanting to scan this neighborhood and hopefully picking up some traces of radiation. But the answer had always been the same.

"We don't have enough to go around. They're all being used at other locations."

He had even called Tyler Wallace, who had promised to scrounge one up and deliver it to him, but so far no luck.

Wallace had asked if he wanted backup. Jacob had told him to hold off for the moment. Sneaking around alone would yield better results.

He crept down the street, peering at each building as he clutched a Beretta M12 submachinegun that a friendly Carabinieri had given him. The short firearm with its foldable stock was perfect for urban combat.

He also had the 9mm pistol Wallace had provided and a couple of tear gas grenades courtesy of some riot police. One cop even gave him some Ibuprofen for his neck.

Everyone had been very helpful, but no one could help him in the situation he was in now. What the hell was he supposed to do? Knock on doors and ask if there was a nuclear device inside?

Then, up ahead, a shadow moved.

Jacob ducked into a doorway and knelt to make himself less visible.

The shadow had been in front of a darkened shopfront. There were streetlights here, but they were infrequent, and cast many shadows behind dumpsters, corners of buildings, and doorways, leaving plenty of places to hide.

The shadow moved again, resolving itself into a tall, slim man.

A man with an assault rifle.

Jacob aimed his own weapon, zeroing in on the man's center mass.

Two more figures appeared, both holding assault rifles.

As they came into the light, Jacob recognized Italian army uniforms.

A patrol. A patrol of half-children.

Because these were obviously raw recruits. None of them looked older than twenty, and they all looked nervous as hell.

"Psst," Jacob whispered.

The young men went prone, pointing their guns everywhere but at him.

"I'm a friend," Jacob whispered. "I'm an American with the CIA. Do any of you speak English?"

"Come out with your hands up!" the lead soldier commanded in English.

"All right, all right. Calm down."

Jacob didn't have time for this, but he also didn't have time to get in a gunfight with some child soldiers.

Setting down his gun, he stepped into the light with his hands in the air.

The trio approached him, guns leveled.

"I have a pass signed by the chief of police and a colonel in the Italian army. Left pocket."

The leader pulled it out, read it by the light of a streetlamp, and visibly relaxed.

Now that he got a good look at them, Jacob's assessment went up. Their shoulder patches bore the insignia of the Alpini, the elite alpine unit of the Italian army. The guys looked fit. They'd have to be to go through that rugged training for mountain warfare.

The question was, how much training had they made it through before the Italian government threw every available uniform at this crisis?

"You see anything?" Jacob asked.

"No," the leader said. "We just got sent out of the barracks an hour ago and told to patrol this neighborhood. We haven't seen anyone on the streets until we bumped into you."

"I haven't seen anything either," Jacob admitted.

"Hold on," the leader said. "I need to radio in every ten minutes. Hopefully the radio will work better here."

The leader got on a walkie-talkie and started speaking in Italian. Jacob retrieved his weapon while the other two took up positions to monitor the street and the upstairs windows. They were alert, he'd give them that.

Then something struck him. He went back to the leader and waited until he finished his report.

"Did you say you had radio trouble?"

"Yeah, about ten minutes ago. I guess the buildings just got in the way."

"But that hadn't happened before?"

"Um, no."

"What kind of trouble did you have?"

"Just static. I could still hear dispatch, but it was pretty noisy."

Jacob took in a sharp breath.

"Show me where this was."

CHAPTER TWENTY SIX

Jana now rode on the back of a different motorcycle, one driven by her dad. As she clutched him around the middle as tightly as her injured shoulder allowed, her broken nose still bleeding freely, she remembered the thrill she felt when he'd take her out for a spin as a little girl. He'd get up to 120 on some highways, and Jana would feel like they were about to take off.

She had spent a long, long time and way too much energy being angry at her father for his frequent absences and faked death, but as she looked back, she saw all that anger and resentment had obscured some good times.

When he had been home, he had been all hers. He'd taught her so much and made her feel like the center of the universe.

Then ruined that feeling by flying off to some strategic crisis point. Again.

She used to call him a "yo-yo parent" to her friends. Never to him. Even as a surly teen, she had realized that wasn't entirely fair. He was protecting the nation, after all.

Now she knew he was protecting the world.

And her. He had learned about a hit squad sent by The Order to target her and Jacob, and not knowing where they were, had tailed the hit squad, knowing they'd lead her right to them.

Her father braked, Jana having to show her pass to yet another roadblock. While the streets had been cleared of traffic and the warnings on all the media had kept most people indoors, these roadblocks were seriously slowing them down.

At least this was the last. They were only a few blocks from the Egyptian Institute. The soldiers waved them through and they sped onwards to the neighborhood.

She hoped Jacob had made it here, and wondered if he had. There wasn't any gunfire or explosions like usual.

"So once we get to the institute, where should we look?" her father called over his shoulder.

"I don't know," Jana admitted. Now that she had made it here, she had no idea how to proceed. She had visions of Jacob wandering around the neighborhood, faced with the same problem.

After a minute, she added, "Let's get to the institute. It's only another couple of blocks. That's where he would have started his search. Once we're there, maybe we can retrace his steps."

***

Jacob and the three Alpini observed the row of houses from a vantage point across the street. They looked like every other row of houses on this fairly prosperous residential street—modern homes big enough to have three or four bedrooms. That meant a hefty price tag in any European capital.

Jacob clutched the Alpinis' walkie-talkie, turned down low in order to not draw attention. Pressed to his ear, he had noticed a rise in static as they drew closer.

Interference because of radiation? Maybe.

They drew back half a block, and the static reduced.

"Let's find a way behind that street. I want to figure out if it's these houses or the ones behind."

One of the young soldiers brought up Google Maps on his phone, and they used that to circle around the houses while remaining out of sight of them. They ended up on another residential street behind the one they had been looking at.

The static was fainter here, but still audible. They began to walk down the street, keeping a sharp watch. No one was out. Had the government issued a stay-at-home order? Jacob hoped so. He had a feeling this was about to get messy.

The hissing on the walkie-talkie began to drown out the radio chatter. It reached a crescendo, then began to fade and the chatter returned.

Jacob and the Alpini retracted their steps.

"It must be this house," one of the mountain soldiers said. "Or the one behind."

Most of the windows of the house they stood in front of had their blinds down, but the living room, facing the street, had their blinds open a crack. Creeping toward the house, they saw an older Italian couple watching television.

They moved around the house, staying silent, and got to the back yard. The hissing grew even louder.

The house right behind the one they had passed had Venetian blinds pulled down on every window, and yet just enough light shone out from around them to tell Jacob that the entire house was lit up.

Who keeps all the lights on in a house that big?

A large group of people, that's who.

Jacob motioned for the Alpini to follow. They hopped over a chest-high brick wall separating the back yards.

The hissing grew even stronger. Jacob turned down the volume a bit.

Huddled in the shadow of a tree, they contemplated their next move.

The back of the house was wide enough to have two rooms side to side. Judging from the pipes leading out below the righthand window of the ground floor, Jacob figured it to be the kitchen. They probably wouldn't build the bomb in the kitchen because it would be a long process, and you needed to feed the team. The lefthand window on the ground floor might be a possibility, but Jacob bet it was upstairs, where any unexpected visitors wouldn't stumble upon it immediately. It gave the terrorists a chance to defend the stairs while they set off the bomb.

Would it be at the back or the front? Probably the back, for more privacy. Even with the blinds drawn, criminals naturally preferred the least exposed room.

So the upper lefthand or righthand window.

He got into a huddle with the three young soldiers. They looked keyed up, ready. Each clutched a Beretta ARX160, a good assault rifle, assuming they could shoot straight.

"You guys ever hear a shot fired in anger?"

"A what?"

"You ever seen combat?"

"No."

Jacob grit his teeth.

"You're trained, though, right?"

"We're almost out of basic training."

I thought you'd say that. I hate it when I'm right.

He pointed to the youngest-looking one in the group. "OK. You take this walkie-talkie and get to someplace where they'll hear you above the static. Call for backup. Then rejoin us. The shooting will have already started, so just come in wherever you think you'll do the most good. You two are with me."

The three teenagers looked at each other nervously.

"You up for it?" Jacob asked.

Their faces hardened. "We all have family here."

"All right. You get out of here. Emphasize to them that we need as much backup as they can spare. We're going in right now. There's no time to waste. As soon as they get that bomb assembled, they'll blow it."

The soldier with the walkie-talkie hurried off, vaulting the brick wall and running away. Jacob turned to the others. Before he could speak, one of them said,

"How do we know this is the right place? Couldn't the interference be from something other than radiation?"

"It could be. So here's what we'll do. You fire at the left window on the upper floor, and you fire at the right. I got two tear gas grenades. When you bust through the glass, I'll throw them in. Then we go through that back door next to the kitchen. If it's civilians, the worst we'll have done is scare the shit out of them."

The two young men nodded.

They got into position. Jacob pulled out both grenades and stood at the ready. He gave the signal.

Both opened up with their assault rifles. Glass shattered and the Venetian blinds danced.

Jacob threw a tear gas grenade into the lefthand window and then turned to do the same with the window on the right …

… and noticed something wrong. The Venetian blinds, battered by the bullets, were jerking but not by much. It looked like it was vibrating.

Hitting some barrier behind it.

"Both of you concentrate full auto on that window!" Jacob shouted. He could hear a ringing of bullets on metal above the gunfire.

Then the Venetian blind fell down to reveal a metal plate behind, perforated by bullet holes.

Oh, Jesus, I bet that's lead.

A moment later the sheet toppled backwards.

Jacob threw the tear gas grenade. Already, the fumes were billowing out the other window.

"Let's get in there!" he shouted the moment the grenade exploded.

They never got the chance. The two ground-floor windows flew open to reveal two men each. All four of them poured fire into the backyard.

One of the Alpini jerked and fell. Jacob and the other young man jumped over the brick wall to take cover.

Jacob moved a bit to one side and popped up to fire his submachinegun and immediately had to duck back down as a storm of lead flew in his direction. The Alpini tried the same tactic and also didn't get a chance to fire.

"We need to get in there!" the kid said.

Jacob didn't see how. There would be terrorists guarding every window and a clear space around the house.

He needed to think of something quick. That tear gas would only stop them from entering the bomb room for only a minute or two.

Jacob spotted an old Fiat in the driveway of the house next door. He grinned at his young comrade-in-arms.

"Keep firing at the house," Jacob told the Alpini. "Shift around a bit, so it looks like we're both still here."

The recruit stared at him.

"And where are you going?"

"To do something stupid."

CHAPTER TWENTY SEVEN

As soon as Jana and her father heard the gunshots, they hopped back on the motorcycle and sped in the direction of the sound. Two explosions followed, and then more gunshots. Some civilians peeked out of their windows, but no one ventured onto the streets.

They ended up on a residential street of large houses. The flare of gunfire told them which house was the center of the action.

That and an old Fiat peeling out of the driveway next door, ending up in the driveway across the street, then reversing.

It blew through the front yard of the target house and slammed right through the front door, taking a large section of wall with it.

"We've found Jacob," Jana said with a smile.

They hopped off the bike. Her dad wielded an MP5, Jacob's favorite weapon. She wondered if that was yet another habit her father passed onto him. Jana had a pair of 9mm pistols, the one Wallace had given her and the other taken off the body of one of her abductors. With the terrorists so occupied by Jacob's grand entrance, they simply ran up the front lawn without any worries.

A terrorist showed himself at an upper window and fell back with a hail of Jana's and her father's bullets.

The Fiat had ended up half in the front hallway, its steaming hood sticking out of the front of the building. Gunfire roared within. Jana and Aaron Peters clambered over the car and heaps of debris to get inside.

They got there just in time to see Jacob running up the stairs, and just in time to shoot a terrorist who had swung around a doorway on the ground floor to aim at his back.

Jacob disappeared upstairs, and for the moment Jana and Aaron had to take cover as the terrorists, having gotten over their initial shock, converged on them through both sides of the house.

The fighting was chaotic. Dust hazed the air from the collision. Overturned furniture and collapsed portions of the ceiling and walls made seeing difficult. Jana smelled something burning, and thought she detected the acrid tang of tear gas.

Jana ended up wedged between a heap of debris that protected her on two sides while leaving her exposed to the stairs and the room to her right. The hallway next to the stairs was too filled with portions of the front wall for anyone to get through. As she exchanged fire with someone in the room to her right, ducking and shooting as he did the same, Jacob reappeared.

Tumbling down the stairs while grappling with Hamza.

Jana fired another couple of shots into the room and scrambled over bits of wood, concrete, and drywall to get to him. Her dad had disappeared somewhere to the left, judging from the sound of gunfire. She heard fire from a couple of assault rifles near the back of the house, too. Had someone else gotten into the game?

She got to Jacob and Hamza, who were punching, kicking, and clawing at each other at the foot of the stairs. She raised one of her guns to pistol whip him.

"The bomb is upstairs to the left!" Jacob shouted in between, getting his face punched.

Jana sprinted upstairs, taking the steps three at a time. Tear gas hung in the air up there, and it was already beginning to burn her lungs and make her eyes water before she made it halfway up.

A man swung around the corner of the top of the stairs, choking and coughing but gun at the ready. Jana didn't even slow down as she shot him.

She rounded the corner to head for the bomb room …

… and got a fist in her face.

The sudden impact on her broken nose was such a shock that she tumbled back, hit the corner of the wall, and rolled several steps down before stopping herself.

She was up again in an instant, stumbled, then finally got her arms and legs coordinated. Jana crawled more than walked up the stairs.

Dr. Moswen Farag stood in the hallway in front of an open doorway. He was coughing despite the handkerchief pressed to his face, and tears poured from his bloodshot eyes. It must have been him who had punched her, but now he didn't seem to notice she'd come back. Even half obscured by the handkerchief and the smoke, she could see he was terrified. He looked like he was trying to psych himself up to go into that room.

With a roar, he jumped up and down three times and then rushed into the room.

But he had hesitated too long. Jana came right after him.

She entered a large room cleared of furniture. Only a large worktable stood in the center with a metal container the size of a truck engine. Lead sheets lined the walls except at the window, where it had been shot out. Two men in Tyvek suits lay dead on the floor from gunshot wounds.

That's all she got to see. Dr. Farag was almost to the bomb. A big red button was set on the side of it. He reached for it.

Jana tackled him. They landed on the floor right at the foot of the worktable.

Dr. Farag struggled, trying to turn over as Jana punched him in the back of the neck. He lashed out with an elbow and hit her square in her shattered nose.

Jana saw stars and toppled backwards. She felt blackness reach up to envelop her …

No! She forced her burning eyes to open and focus.

Dr. Farag had gotten to his feet and was reaching for the button.

She lashed out with both legs, hitting the back of his knees and making him fall right onto her.

Jana let out a gust of breath as his heavy weight slammed into her chest. Her next inhalation was pure fire. She could hardly see now, hardly breathe, but then again neither could he.

She got him in a chokehold, pressing one arm around his neck from behind while gripping her own wrist with her free hand and pulling it back to increase the pressure.

He struggled, lashing out, but she had him in a good position. All she had to do was not fall unconscious before he did.

Her coughs came continuously now, wracking her body as she struggled with the man who had once been her colleague and had become her enemy. Her vision blurred, and she shut her eyes out of pure agony.

But still, she held on. As she wavered between consciousness and darkness, she continued to press against the doctor's neck. His struggles grew weak, then he went still.

She kept her grip until she heard heavy footsteps enter the room.

Jana cried out, pushed Dr. Farag's body off her, and launched herself at the newcomer.

She ended up wrapping her arms around Jacob's legs.

"Easy there," he said. "Easy. We got 'em. We 'em all."

Jana sank back down to the floor and into blissful oblivion.

***

As Jana and Jacob sat in the back of an Italian ambulance parked a couple of blocks away from the terrorist safehouse, Tyler Wallace debriefed them. Aaron stood outside, still alert, still on the watch.

"Good news from the emergency response crew," Wallace said. "It looks like the radiation level, while enough to detect through interference on that walkie-talkie, wasn't a lethal dose."

Jana let out a sigh of relief. “Good thing they had a thick casing on that thing. Some of the bullets Jacob shot inside that room ricocheted off it.”

Jacob gave a shrug. “Those ricochets killed the engineers. Now, about those radiation levels … ”

“You weren’t exposed to it for long,” Wallace replied. “They’re going to take you to the hospital now and give you some treatments that will help your body flush out the radiation. You shouldn’t have any short-term effects.”

“And long-term effects?” Jana asked.

Wallace grimaced and shrugged. “Better ask the doctors about that.”

She thought of cancer, and the risk of having children, and found that she couldn’t care much about herself considering the disaster they had just averted.

“We’ll just have to deal with it,” Jana said in a small voice.

Wallace looked at her for a moment, then said, “You did some damn good work here today. All of you.”

“There are more fights to come,” Aaron said, still watching the street.

“I know,” Wallace said. “But we’ll soon have another weapon against them.”

“What’s that?” Jacob asked.

"The mole. We haven't found him or her yet, but we know there's a mole. I'm working on a plan to figure out who it is."

“How?” Jacob asked.

"I've started laying little traps to see if any of my inner circle would slip up and reveal themselves. I've eliminated a couple of suspects already, and one by one, I'll eliminate them all until there's only one left, and God help that one."

“How do you plan to do that?” Aaron asked.

“I’m faking calls from Jacob. I use AI to match his voice and make the computer call my phone when certain people in my inner circle are with me. I play like I don’t want the others to hear, but let out just enough information to give them something juicy to pass onto our enemies, then I monitor their movements and calls."

Jacob let out a long, low whistle. "You're a crafty one."

Wallace smiled. "That's why I'm your boss."

"Even if you find the mole, they might not know much," Aaron said. "The Order has a cell structure and their security is tighter than any I've ever seen."

"It's a start," Wallace said. "And now that you're back in the loop, I think we can make some real inroads."

Aaron gave him a somber nod.

A couple of young Italian soldiers came up to the ambulance.

"Hey guys," Jacob said. He turned to the others. "These are the Alpini that alerted me to the radiation interference on their walkie-talkie. And they came into the fight too, charged right through the back door and blew away a couple of terrorists."

"Good job," Wallace said.

"I wished I could have seen it," Jana said, "but I was pretty much out of it by then."

"Giuseppe didn't make it," one of them said, his voice breaking.

"Was that your friend who help shoot out the windows?"

They nodded.

Jacob climbed out of the ambulance, stiff and wincing with pain. He put a hand on each of the young man's shoulders.

"He died a hero. There's going to be a monument to him in this neighborhood. A monument for all three of you. You weren't even out of basic training, and you helped save your nation. Mourn your friend, but be proud of him too. He died for the principles he signed up for."

They nodded sadly.

"You should have the monument," one of them said. "You and your friends. You did more than we did."

Jacob smiled. "People like us don't get monuments."

"What's your name?" the Italian asked.

"We don't have names, either. But you might see us again. If you two keep fighting the way you fought tonight, we might be colleagues one day."

Jacob shook hands with the two soldiers, then climbed back into the ambulance. The sirens switched on, and the ambulance made its way through the crowd of police and army vehicles on its way to the hospital.

NOW AVAILABLE!

TARGET EIGHT
(The Spy Game—Book #8)

"Thriller writing at its best... A gripping story that's hard to put down."
--Midwest Book Review, Diane Donovan (re *Any Means Necessary*)

From #1 bestselling and USA Today bestselling author Jack Mars, author of the critically acclaimed *Luke Stone* and *Agent Zero* series (with over 5,000 five-star reviews), comes an explosive new action-packed espionage series that takes readers on a wild ride across Europe, America, and the world—perfect for fans of Dan Brown, Daniel Silva and Jack Carr.

When terrorists threaten to blow up a major dam, threatening one of the world's most important archeological sites, Jacob is summoned to find them and stop them before it's too late. But in a series of never-ending twists and turns, Jacob learns that finding them won't be as easy as it seems—and that their ultimate target may be even worse than thought…

An unputdownable action thriller with heart-pounding suspense and unforeseen twists, TARGET EIGHT is the eighth novel in an exhilarating new series by a #1 bestselling author that will make you fall in love with a brand-new action hero—and keep you turning pages late into the night.

Future books in the series will soon be available.

"One of the best thrillers I have read this year. The plot is intelligent and will keep you hooked from the beginning. The author did a superb job creating a set of characters who are fully developed and very much enjoyable. I can hardly wait for the sequel."
--Books and Movie Reviews, Roberto Mattos (re Any Means Necessary)

Jack Mars

Jack Mars is the USA Today bestselling author of the LUKE STONE thriller series, which includes seven books. He is also the author of the new FORGING OF LUKE STONE prequel series, comprising six books; of the AGENT ZERO spy thriller series, comprising twelve books; of the TROY STARK thriller series, comprising five books; and of the SPY GAME thriller series, comprising nine books.

Jack loves to hear from you, so please feel free to visit www.Jackmarsauthor.com to join the email list, receive a free book, receive free giveaways, connect on Facebook and Twitter, and stay in touch!

BOOKS BY JACK MARS

THE SPY GAME
TARGET ONE (Book #1)
TARGET TWO (Book #2)
TARGET THREE (Book #3)
TARGET FOUR (Book #4)
TARGET FIVE (Book #5)
TARGET SIX (Book #6)
TARGET SEVEN (Book #7)
TARGET EIGHT (Book #8)
TARGET NINE (Book #9)

TROY STARK THRILLER SERIES
ROGUE FORCE (Book #1)
ROGUE COMMAND (Book #2)
ROGUE TARGET (Book #3)
ROGUE MISSION (Book #4)
ROGUE SHOT (Book #5)

LUKE STONE THRILLER SERIES
ANY MEANS NECESSARY (Book #1)
OATH OF OFFICE (Book #2)
SITUATION ROOM (Book #3)
OPPOSE ANY FOE (Book #4)
PRESIDENT ELECT (Book #5)
OUR SACRED HONOR (Book #6)
HOUSE DIVIDED (Book #7)

FORGING OF LUKE STONE PREQUEL SERIES
PRIMARY TARGET (Book #1)
PRIMARY COMMAND (Book #2)
PRIMARY THREAT (Book #3)
PRIMARY GLORY (Book #4)
PRIMARY VALOR (Book #5)
PRIMARY DUTY (Book #6)

AN AGENT ZERO SPY THRILLER SERIES

AGENT ZERO (Book #1)
TARGET ZERO (Book #2)
HUNTING ZERO (Book #3)
TRAPPING ZERO (Book #4)
FILE ZERO (Book #5)
RECALL ZERO (Book #6)
ASSASSIN ZERO (Book #7)
DECOY ZERO (Book #8)
CHASING ZERO (Book #9)
VENGEANCE ZERO (Book #10)
ZERO ZERO (Book #11)
ABSOLUTE ZERO (Book #12)

Made in United States
North Haven, CT
18 June 2024

53802300R00100